L. D. KNORR

Dead Catch

The RV Mysteries
Book THREE

Dead Catch

For information about special discounts for bulk purchases, please contact Sunbury Press, Inc. Wholesale Dept. at (855) 338-8359 or orders@sunburypress.com.

To request one of our authors for speaking engagements or book signings, please contact Sunbury Press, Inc. Publicity Dept. at publicity@sunburypress.com.

FIRST SUNBURY PRESS EDITION
Printed in the United States of America
November 2013

Trade Paperback ISBN: 978-1-62006-275-3
Mobipocket format (Kindle) ISBN: 978-1-62006-276-0
ePub format (Nook) ISBN: 978-1-62006-277-7

Published by:
Sunbury Press
Mechanicsburg, PA
www.sunburypress.com

Mechanicsburg, Pennsylvania   USA

Acknowledgments

Thank you to my editor Jennifer Melendrez who corrected the thousand and one punctuation errors and whose suggestions made it a far better book.

Thanks to my wife Emily for making vital suggestions for the book and for tolerating my full-time retired presence while I commandeered a corner of our living room for my portable writing desk.

Thank you Sunbury Press for publishing my work.

And last but not least, a salute to all the millions of RVers across the country seeking adventure. I wish you smooth highways and level campsites.

Chapter 1

Helen had no sooner ended the call from Rolf Kramden when the phone rang again. She recognized the number of her daughter, Ali, who lived in Shreveport along with their son-in-law, Preston, and their grandson, Chip. "Hello, Ali."

"Mom! Are you and Dad OK? Why didn't you call to let us know what happened? I had to hear about it on CNN! The last time we talked, you and Dad were heading to a dinner cruise with Senator Westbrook."

"I'm sorry, Ali. We should have called but things were happening so fast and we were so caught up in them that we just plain forgot. I was going to call you this afternoon after we put Michigan behind us."

"Where are you now?"

"We are on Interstate 80 in Ohio, close to the border of Pennsylvania."

"Were you and Dad hurt during the senator's attempted murder?

"No, sweetheart, we are just fine. The only casualty was the outfit that I wore to the senator's dinner cruise, but Mrs. Westbrook was kind enough to replace it."

"Well, from now on call us every day to let us know you are both still alive. I worry about you all the time driving that big motorhome around even without you both getting into trouble."

"Quit worrying about your dad driving the motorhome. He's made it look so easy that I am going to try driving it soon."

"That's something you didn't need to tell me, mother. You're not really planning to drive that rig, are you?"

"No, not on this trip. I want to practice around home first."

"Well, at least I don't have to worry about that yet."

"Ali, quit your worrying. We should be fine the rest of the trip. We will spend a few days in Pennsylvania Amish

Country and then head to Washington for dinner at the White House with the president and Senator Westbrook."

"YOU ARE HAVING DINNER AT THE WHITE HOUSE?!"

"Yes, we are! Senator Westbrook is good friends with the president. He said the president wants to meet us, so he invited us to the White House for dinner. He wants to hear firsthand about your dad's rescue of the senator. We'll tell you all about it when we get home."

The Morans, recently involved in the rescue of Michigan Senator Kenton Westbrook from the Grand River in Lansing, Michigan, began their involvement with the senator while traveling north from Kenner Louisiana where Hank Moran, a recently retired robbery/homicide detective, and his wife, Helen, were setting out on a month long tour in their new motorhome. While stopped at an Indiana rest area, Hank witnessed the murder of a Hispanic American man named Agusto Soto. The murder was a hate crime perpetrated by a member of a white supremacist Michigan militia.

Hank and Helen, aided by veteran Lansing newspaper reporter Rolf Kramden, investigated the Soto murder. During their investigation, they discovered a plot by the militant militia to squelch, by murder if necessary, new firearms legislation that was proposed by Senator Westbrook. A confrontation between Senator Westbrook and the militia leader aboard the *Lansing Princess* riverboat led to the attempted murder of the senator. The senator was knocked unconscious and dumped overboard into the Grand River and subsequently rescued by Hank.

Hank motioned to Helen and said, "Put the call on the speaker."

"Hold on, Ali, I'm going to put us on the speakerphone. Your dad wants to talk to you."

"Hi, Ali, I was wondering if Chip has any long weekends off from school next month. I was thinking about taking him over to Lake Claiborne on a little fishing trip."

"Hi, Dad, I think that would be great. I'll check his school schedule. All he talks about is taking a camping trip in the motorhome with Gramma and Grampa."

"OK, we'll put that into our plans when we get back home. I wanted to get a lot of practice in driving the rig before we take him along with us."

"I'll let Chip know. I'm sure he'll be excited. In the meantime, keep Mom out of trouble."

"I think you should be telling your mother to keep *me* out of trouble after the way she handled herself the other night."

"OK then, y'all keep *each other* out of trouble, and call us at least once a day to let us know you are safe. I have to go now. The oven just beeped."

"OK, Ali, we'll call you soon. Love you, bye."

Helen had called ahead and made a reservation for one night at the Kozy Rest Campground, ten miles off of Interstate 80, northeast of Pittsburgh. As they were approaching the campground on the narrow two–lane, tree-lined road, a huge low-flying bird carrying a spotted fawn in its talons headed directly toward the front of their motorhome.

"Holy cow! Did you see that!?" Helen exclaimed.

"How could I miss it?" Hank replied. "It barely cleared the top of the Bounder! I thought it was going to crash into our windshield. I did hear a thump up on the roof."

"What was it?" Helen asked. "I've never seen a bird that big."

"It looked like a huge brown eagle. I've seen Bald Eagles while fishing down on the bayou. This one looked to be half again their size. Its wingspan was nearly as wide as the road!"

"When we get up to the campground we'll have to ask about it," Helen replied.

"And I better check up top to see if there's any damage."

Hank pulled into the campground and parked the motorhome in the designated lane for new registrants. When he and Helen entered the campground office they noticed a small group of people sitting in the lounge area. Some of the group had binoculars hanging from straps around their necks. Two men in the group wore African bush hats.

As they approached the counter the clerk said, "Good afternoon, welcome to Kozy Rest. My name is Margie. How can I help you?"

"Hello, Margie. We have a reservation for one night," Hank said. "The name is Moran."

"Yes, here you are," the clerk said when she found the reservation on her computer. "You are staying for one night and requested a pull-thru site."

"That is correct, ma'am," Hank replied.

After Hank paid the fee, Margie told them that she would escort them to their site.

"By the way," Hank said, "you have awfully large birds in this part of the country. One nearly flew into our rig carrying a small deer in its talons."

Upon hearing Hank's remark the small group instantly became quiet. One of the men who were wearing the African bush hats, a small wiry looking man with round lens wire rimmed glasses, approached Hank. "Sir, did I just hear you say you saw a large bird carrying a deer?"

"Yes, we did," Hank replied. We saw it about a half mile down the road from the campground entrance. It barely cleared the top of our motorhome."

"What did the bird look like?" the man excitedly asked.

"Well, it was definitely some kind of eagle. It was brown with yellow legs and had huge talons that gripped the deer."

"About how big was the bird?"

"It's hard to say. It all happened so fast. But I did notice that its wingspan was nearly as wide as the road."

Hank's last comment about the bird's wingspan sent a loud murmur through the group.

"Sir, our group is from the Western Pennsylvania Audubon Society. We are in the area because of recent sightings of the bird that you just mentioned."

"If you're from the Audubon Society then you should be able to tell us what we saw," Hank replied.

"If what you say is accurate, you are two of the very few lucky people who just happened to see a Washington's

Eagle. Sightings have occurred in this area every few years since the time of Audubon in the nineteenth century."

"Then what you are saying is ... this bird is rare," Helen said.

"Yes, ma'am. The Washington Eagle is extremely rare. Some ornithologists claim it doesn't even exist. John James Audubon actually shot one and described it fully in his notes. He even produced one of his now famous paintings of it. Later they tried to discredit Audubon saying no such bird could exist—that it was only an immature bald eagle. I have a copy of that painting on my laptop. Please let me show it to you."

The man went back to his seat in the lounge and booted up his laptop. "Ah, here it is," he said as he approached Hank and Helen. "Take a look at this picture."

Hank and Helen both scrutinized the picture and agreed that the bird they saw looked very much like the one in Audubon's painting.

"Now, which way was the bird heading when you saw it?" the man asked.

"Like I said, it flew right over us from the front as we were approaching the campground, so it would have been heading west," Hank replied. "I don't think it could have flown very far considering the size of the deer that it was carrying."

The man heartily thanked Hank and Helen and returned to the group. In an instant the group was out the door and seconds later Hank heard three vehicles tear out of the campground.

"I guess they're pretty excited about that bird," Hank said to Margie the clerk.

"They have been here for most of a week trying to get a glimpse of that bird, and you two just happen to drive up and have it almost go through your windshield," Margie replied with a chuckle.

"I guess we're just lucky," Hank replied.

"Well, folks, I'll escort you to your site now."

After Hank had the Bounder parked and leveled and the water, sewer, and power lines connected, he climbed the rear ladder to inspect the roof of the motorhome. The only sign of a collision was a mark on the front of the forward rooftop air conditioner housing. He guessed that a dangling foot of the unfortunate deer struck the housing. Upon further inspection he found a large brown feather wedged under the front of the housing. Satisfied that there was no other damage to the Bounder he made his way back down the ladder and hopped off the rear bumper.

"Did you find any damage up on the roof?" Helen asked when he was back on the ground.

"No damage that I could see, just a mark on the front of the AC housing. And I found this feather, too."

"Oh, Hank, if that is a feather from that bird it could be very valuable to science!"

"Yeah, I thought the same thing. We should give it to that group when they return from their little excursion. They should be able to get decent DNA test results from it."

"Good idea!" Helen replied. "I'll get one of my large plastic bags to keep it in!"

Helen went into the Bounder and came back out with the largest baggie she could find. Only half of the feather fit into the bag with a good twelve inches protruding out the top.

Later that evening, Hank and Helen sat outside to enjoy the cool evening breeze. Helen was enjoying a glass of chardonnay and Hank was sipping from a longneck bottle of Pabst Blue Ribbon when they saw the three vehicles of the Audubon group return. The small man Hank had talked to earlier pulled up in front of a white Fleetwood class C motorhome two sites down and across the drive. In a short while the rest of the group joined the man on the patio of his site.

Hank and Helen, carrying the baggie that contained the feather, walked across the drive and approached the group.

"Good evening, folks," Hank said. "Did you have any luck in spotting that big bird?"

"No, none at all," the man dejectedly replied. "It's probably over in Mercer County by now."

"We have something here that you might be interested in," Helen said. "My husband found this feather up on the roof of our motorhome. It most likely came from that large eagle."

Helen handed the bag to the man and he reached for it with a trembling hand. He gingerly removed the feather from the plastic bag and quickly examined it.

"This is definitely a primary wing feather," he stated. "From just the size of this feather I can tell it came from no known species of raptor. The largest primary wing feathers from known eagles range from sixteen to twenty-two inches in length. This one must be twenty-six inches. May I please keep it?" The man excitedly asked. "We need to take it back to Pittsburgh and have a thorough DNA test performed on it."

"I thought you might want to do that," Hank replied. "You are more than welcome to the feather."

"Here we are most likely making ornithological history and I haven't even introduced myself. I am Harold Parkinson, president of the Western Pennsylvania Audubon Society. And these people are all members of the society."

As Hank shook Parkinson's hand he said, "I am Hank Moran and this is my wife, Helen."

A lady from the front of the group, dressed head to toe in a camouflage outfit, stepped forward and introduced herself. "My name is Ruth Benson. I am secretary of the society. Your names sound so familiar. I know I just heard your names somewhere very recently."

"You might have heard our names on CNN the past few days," Helen replied. "We just came from a little adventure up in Michigan."

"Yes! That's it!" Ruth replied. "Mr. Moran, you are the man that rescued the Michigan senator from the river and, Mrs. Moran, you were kidnapped by that awful militia man."

"That was us," Helen replied.

"Harold, these people are celebrities—and staying here at the same campground!" Ruth declared.

The rest of the group came to life and they all introduced themselves to the Morans.

"Mr. and Mrs. Moran," Harold began, "I need your address and phone number as references for the paper I intend to write if the DNA tests on the feather prove the bird is an unknown. We won't be able to say it was a Washington's Eagle because we have nothing to compare the results to. However your eyewitness account combined with the tests would make us one step closer to proving its existence. Your address and phone number will not be made public. However, you may be contacted by officials from the national office."

"That is just fine, Mr. Parkinson," Hank replied. "I hope the tests confirm your suspicions that the feather might belong to the Washington's Eagle."

"Like I said, the mere size of the feather leads us assuredly in that direction," Harold said with satisfaction.

Hank gave Harold Parkinson their pertinent contact information then bid the group goodnight.

As Hank and Helen were walking back to their motorhome Hank said, "Well, finding rare eagle feathers is a heck of a lot more fun than jumping off of riverboats."

"The worst that could have happened was a cracked windshield instead of a cracked head," Helen replied.

They both laughed as they entered the Bounder.

Chapter 2

The next morning the Morans were back on the road by nine a.m. and cruising Interstate 80 through scenic Central Pennsylvania. They turned south on US 11 and followed the Susquehanna River south to Harrisburg, the state capital. One hour later, in mid-afternoon, they pulled into the Old Mill Stream Campground just off Route 30 in Lancaster County, the heart of the Pennsylvania Amish farm country.

Being mid-September, they had no problem in securing a large pull-thru site. The summer rush was over and families no longer flocked to the Dutch Wonderland Amusement Park, which was located adjacent to the campground.

As Hank was checking in, Helen browsed the racks full of tourist information and pamphlets. They had three days to explore the area before they had to leave for D.C. and dinner at the White House.

It was at the Kitchen Kettle Village in the nearby town of Intercourse that Hank had his first taste of wet bottom shoofly pie. After a one hour buggy ride through Amish farm country, Hank went back into the store and bought a whole pie to take back to their campsite.

They spent the next three days exploring the Amish way of life that Helen found so fascinating while reading the *Heritage of Lancaster County Series* books. Their sightseeing included an informative afternoon at the Amish Village in the town of Ronks.

They were driving through the quaint town of Bird-in-Hand when Hank spied the Bird-in-Hand Bakeshop and pulled into the parking lot. "Why are we stopping here?" Helen asked.

"I decided a taste test had to be performed to determine which shop made the best wet bottom shoofly pie," Hank responded.

"Well, I've been told that the best shoofly pies are made at the Dutch Haven Bakery," Helen added.

"Good, we can stop there also on the way back to the campground. A thorough investigation is warranted!"

"Hank, we're both going to gain twenty pounds before we leave Lancaster County!"

"We can walk it off exploring Washington in a few days," Hank replied.

Helen found a small round Distlefink hex sign at the Bird-in-Hand farmers market. The Distlefink, or thistle finch, is the good luck bird of the Pennsylvania Dutch. Helen decided to hang it inside the kitchen window of the motorhome thinking they needed all of the good luck they could garner considering the harrowing events of the past six weeks.

With the exploration of Amish country accomplished and parts of three equally delicious shoofly pies in the freezer, Hank headed the motorhome down I-83 past York, to Baltimore, then south on I-95 to the Cherry Hill Park campground in College Park, Maryland. The campground, conveniently located on the D.C. beltway with Metro bus service available to the nearest Metro-Rail station, was only a short train ride from the National Mall.

After checking in and hooking the Bounder up to the utilities, Hank called Senator Westbrook to inform him of their arrival. The senator's secretary routed him to Westbrook's cell phone.

"Hello, Senator. Hank Moran. We're here in Washington."

"Hank, glad you could make it! Are you and Helen all set for tomorrow evening?

"I'm not quite sure. What is the dress code for dinner at the White House?"

"A coat and tie will be fine, Hank. The president likes to keep these affairs as informal as possible. He likes to relax and enjoy the company."

"That's good to hear. I thought I would have to go out and rent a tux. OK, now that that's settled, how do we get there? We're at the Cherry Hill Park campground up in College Park."

"I'll have my driver pick you up at the campground at six, then swing around to pick up Clarice and me. We should make it to the White House just before seven."

"OK, Senator, we'll see you then."

"No tux required, Helen. Only a coat and tie."

"Well, you are *not* going to wear that old rag that you brought along," Helen replied. "We need to go shopping to get you a new suit. I was thinking I should get a new dress for the occasion, too. I don't want to wear slacks to the White House."

A short hop on the beltway to North Bethesda and the White Flint Mall solved both of their wardrobe needs. Helen found a basic black V-neck sheath dress and a simple white pearl necklace at the Talbots store. A short distance down the mall, at the Men's Wearhouse, Helen approved of Hank's appearance in a charcoal multi-stripe suit, blue shirt, and maroon and gray paisley tie.

"Oh my, I forgot how handsome you look in a good suit and tie!" Helen exclaimed.

"It's been quite a while, but I have to admit I do clean up pretty good," Hank replied with a smile as he admired his own image in the full length mirror.

At five minutes to six the next evening, Hank received a call from the campground office that a limousine was there to pick them up. Hank said to send it on down to their site. The appearance of the sleek black limo and driver produced a few stares from fellow campers lounging outside of their RVs. The driver, dressed in black slacks and short sleeved white shirt, exited the limo and said, "Good evening, folks, my name is Hannah. I am Senator Westbrook's driver. Are you ready to go to the White House?" Hannah had spoken loud enough for the neighbors to hear and Helen heard a few murmurs among the now attentive loungers.

"We're ready," Hank said as Hannah opened the rear door of the limo.

Forty-five minutes later, after a stop for the Westbrooks and a thorough security search by two secret service agents, the two couples were welcomed to the Executive Mansion by President Robinson and First Lady Marsha Robinson. President Robinson was the first African American to hold the office of president. The Morans were also introduced to FBI director Ted Kunzler and his wife, Anna.

Ten minutes later, Hank and Helen were surprised and delighted to see Rolf Kramden and his fiancée, Linda Hartman, being escorted in to join them in the family dining room on the State Floor of the Executive Mansion. Rolf was the newspaper reporter who played an important role in the solving of the rest area murder that occurred in Indiana. Through a series of events, the murder led to Hank's rescuing of Senator Westbrook from the Grand River in Lansing, Michigan.

President Robinson was anxious to hear the story firsthand from the participants. "OK, I believe everyone is here, let's be seated," the president said.

During the family-style dinner of roast beef, mashed potatoes, and vegetables from the White House garden, and with President Robinson's prompting, the dinner guests related the entire story behind the rescue of Senator Westbrook and Helen's ordeal with the wayward militia.

The First Lady was highly intrigued by Helen's account of her extraordinary escape from the CCB militia kidnappers while Hank was rescuing the senator.

Director Kunzler spoke, "Mr. President, Mr. Moran was also credited with solving the Leviticus murders that occurred this past summer down in Florida, Mississippi, and Tennessee."

"I had a briefing about those murders," President Robinson said. "Please refresh my memory."

"We should let Mr. Moran tell the story," Kunzler replied as he motioned to Hank to take the floor.

Hank began, "The case involving the murder of gay men revolved around an overzealous preacher by the name of Billy Brantley, his twin brother Franklin Whitehead, and their step-brother Calvin Bixler. Brantley and Whitehead were separated at birth, thus the different last names.

Reverend Brantley's troubles began when he became irate at a church council meeting after they decided to open the congregation to gays in order to supplement the church's dwindling attendance. The council fired Brantley from his position reasoning that he would no longer be compatible with their progressive ideas. Brantley then embarked on a mission to literally follow the demands of God as stated in the book of Leviticus to put homosexuals to death. He committed the first murder in Gulf Breeze Florida and under his influence Calvin Bixler committed the murders in Biloxi and Chattanooga."

"I remember from a terrorist briefing that there was also an explosion at a gay men's resort in Tennessee," President Robinson added.

"You are correct, Mr. President." Hank continued. "Bixler, with the aid of Whitehead, who was an explosives expert, tried to set off a bomb in the resort's heavily occupied tavern. Along with agents from the Knoxville FBI office, I found and diffused the bomb. Bixler, after writing a note of confession blew himself up in his RV trailer. Whitehead was located, arrested, and is awaiting trial. Brantley escaped, fled the country, and is presently being sought by the FBI."

"That's quite an impressive story, Mr. Moran," President Robinson stated. "It lends additional credence to what I'm about to do."

Hank was overwhelmed when the president bid him to stand beside him in front of the dining room's ornate fireplace. With the White House photographer snapping pictures and to the applause of all the guests, President Robinson presented Hank with the President's Citizen's Medal for exemplary deeds or services for his country or fellow citizens.

The next afternoon, as promised, Helen called their daughter, Ali. When Ali picked up her phone she excitedly blurted, "Mom, I saw Dad's picture in the paper this morning with the president giving him the award and shaking his hand. We're all so proud of him. I want to hear all about the dinner."

"I'll tell you all about it when we get back home, Ali. We are going to spend a few days seeing the sights in Washington and then we have to stop in Knoxville to give a deposition for the Whitehead trial. We should be back in Kenner in about ten days."

"Good, that will fit into Chip's school schedule just fine. He has a three day weekend coming up in mid-October. He's already getting his fishing gear ready."

"That's great to hear. I'm glad Chip is excited about the camping trip. I'll let your dad know."

"OK, Mom, keep in touch and we'll see you soon."

Four days later, the Morans exited the Metro transit bus at the stop in front of the campground. "Well, that's it for D.C. on this trip," Hank said as they walked back to their motorhome.

"I would have liked to spend more time in the Smithsonian," Helen replied. "I think we would need about a week just to see all of that. We'll have to put another stop in Washington into a future itinerary."

"Maybe we could stop here again on a trip up to Maine and Prince Edward Island," Hank added. "Right now we need to get down to Knoxville to give that deposition and then head home for a while. I was also thinking about applying for my Louisiana private investigator license."

"You could hand out cards like that old TV gunslinger show only have them read: HAVE RV—WILL TRAVEL," Helen jokingly replied.

"Hey, not a bad idea," Hank replied laughing.

During their brief stay in Knoxville to give their deposition for the Franklin Whitehead trial, they were glad to learn from FBI Agent Chris Emory that Agent Crawford had fully recovered from the knock on the head inflicted by the defendant. Agent Crawford was also nearly beaned on the head by Helen with a cast iron skillet when she thought he was a gunman lying in wait for Hank. Whitehead was accused of aiding in the attempt to blow up a tavern in a nearby gay men's resort.

They were also pleased to learn that Reverend Billy Brantley was now in custody in Florida for the murder of a gay man by the name of Lutz. The reunion of the twins and the finding of their mentally ill cousin/step-brother led to the bizarre series of events that left the cousin dead and the brothers in custody.

When the Morans arrived back home in Kenner, Louisiana and walked into their house Hank remarked how large it seemed. "Wow, this place seems huge after spending over a month in the Bounder."

"Well, we really didn't miss the size while we were traveling in the motorhome," Helen replied. I can see now how some people can give up a permanent home and go full-time in an RV."

"We might consider that in the future, but right now I wouldn't want to give up our home base. I think we would need to be on the road a while longer before we were experienced enough to make a decision like that," Hank added.

"Have you made up your mind about applying for a P.I. license? I imagine you would need a home base office if you become a private investigator."

"I am going to send for an application first thing in the morning," Hank replied. "Having been a qualified police officer in the state I am not required to take the training course but I still need to take the two hour test. I am sure I need a physical address in the state to apply for an agency license."

"Where do you send in the application?"

"The board that handles it is up in Baton Rouge."

"How long does the process take?" Helen asked.

"If all goes well I should be in business by Thanksgiving," Hank replied.

"I'll tell you what, since I need to spend the whole day tomorrow catching up on laundry, why don't you just drive up there to fill out the application? You might speed up the process and save a week or two."

"If you're sure you don't mind, I'll do that."

"No, I don't mind. Anyways, I need to get you out from underfoot so I can get my work done, sweetheart. Then we need to get ready to pick up Chip this weekend."

"OK, sounds like a deal. In the meantime I'll go ahead and make reservations up at the state park," Hank replied.

The next day Hank drove the sixty miles to Baton Rouge and found the Louisiana State Board of Private Investigator Examiners on Silverside Drive. He presented his post academy certificate and history of employment with the Kenner Police department and a request to be exempt from the forty hour PI training course. He was told that the board would perform a background check and then if his exemption was approved he would be eligible to take the PI test. Upon a satisfactory test grade he would then be allowed to submit his application for his agency license.

After shelling out thirty dollars for a PI Test Study Manual he was on his way back home.

Helen heard him come in as she was sorting wash in the laundry room. "How did it go up in the capital, Hank?"

He replied, "Not too bad," as he appeared in the doorway. "I bought a study manual to prepare for the test and should be cleared to take it in about two weeks. After I pass the test it's just a matter of waiting for the board to approve my application. I couldn't get a clear answer from the administrator on how long that would take, but knowing how bureaucracies work it could take another month."

"Well, let's just think positive that we'll be celebrating the creation of the Moran Investigations Agency at Thanksgiving dinner," Helen added.

Thursday morning, Hank and Helen set off on the seven hour run up to Shreveport. The motorhome was lightly packed for the weekend fishing trip with their grandson, Chip. Their excitement about taking Chip on his first outing with them in the RV was only exceeded by Chip's. He had been glued to the front window since arriving home from school, anticipating the arrival of the large motorhome that would soon fill up the front driveway.

"Here they are, Mom," he hollered as he went charging out the front door to meet his grandparents.

The door to the motorhome opened and Helen came out first and gave Chip a big hug and kiss. Hank was right behind and followed suit with even bigger hug that lifted the sandy haired lad off the ground.

"Can I see inside?" Chip excitedly asked.

"Sure, go on in," Helen answered. "We'll give you a tour of your home for the next three days."

"Wow, this thing is huge!" Chip exclaimed as he stood in awe and peered around the inside of the Bounder. "Where's my bed?" he asked.

Helen showed him how the sofa pulled out and transformed into a bed.

"Hey, cool. Can I sleep out here tonight?" he asked.

"You sure can," Hank replied. "We need to get an early start for the lake in the morning so let's get your gear loaded."

Preston arrived home from work at five-thirty and greeted his in-laws. "Where's the Honda? I thought you pulled that on behind the motorhome."

"We didn't see any need for it on this trip," Hank replied. "Everything we need is packed inside except the fish bait. That and the boat rental are within walking distance from the camping area."

At dinner that evening Helen related all their adventures regarding the rescue of Senator Westbrook and their dinner at the White House, where Hank was awarded the President's Citizen's Medal. Chip said that he used the story from the newspaper about Grampa as a show-and-tell in school. He was proud that he received an 'A' for the presentation.

Preston voiced concern about his in-laws' proclivity for involvement in strange adventures with Chip in their care for the weekend. Chip said, "Don't worry, Dad, I'll keep Gramma and Grampa out of trouble. We're only going to do some fishing."

Chip's remark produced chuckles around the table and had the immediate effect of dispelling any second thoughts in Preston's mind about the weekend outing.

Since Chip was spending the night out in the Bounder, Hank and Helen opted to do the same instead of using the guest bedroom where they normally slept when visiting their daughter. This meant retiring early, as Chip's bedtime was nine o'clock. This was agreeable with Hank and Helen, as they were a bit tired from the long drive up from Kenner.

Chapter 3

The next morning as Ali was seeing them off, Helen could tell that she was still concerned about letting Chip go with them. She also knew her daughter was anticipating the rare weekend alone with her husband.

"Ya'll be careful, now," Ali beckoned.

"You and Preston be careful, too, this weekend," Helen said with a wink. "On second thought, I take that back. You know I still want a granddaughter to spoil."

"Mom, you're incorrigible!"

The forty mile trip to Lake Claiborne State Park took over an hour and a half as they had to contend with the morning commuter traffic around Shreveport. Chip had a bird's eye view sitting up in the co-pilot seat while Helen sat behind Hank on the sofa. Chip's excitement grew when they finally pulled through the entrance to the state park. The park had only water and electric hookups at the RV sites but if they used the campground facilities as much as possible they wouldn't have to empty the holding tanks until they pulled out on Sunday afternoon.

"Grampa, are we going to get some fishing in this afternoon?" Chip asked anxiously.

"We need to set up the campsite first, have some lunch, and then I thought we would try out the fishing pier first," Hank replied.

"Well, I am getting hungry. What's for lunch?"

"I can see now that he takes after his Grampa," Helen offered. "How do some grilled hamburgers sound, Chip?"

"Alright Gramma, I'll help Grampa set up the grill."

"When are we going to get the boat, Grampa?" Chip asked as they walked down to the fishing pier after lunch.

"I have a canoe reserved for tomorrow, Chip," Hank replied. "I thought we could use live bait to fish from the pier, and then tomorrow we'll toss some artificial lures from the canoe. How does that sound?"

"OK, Grampa. I have some new lures Dad bought for me at the Bass Pro store. The guy at the store said they were the hot new lures that all the pros are using."

"Well, this is a good lake to test them on. I know a secret spot back in the first cove just west of the boat ramp. I used to take your mother there when she was about your age and we always caught lots of fish. We'll try that first in the morning."

"Did my mom really catch fish?"

"Sure, she was good at it, too. She always wound up catching more than me."

"I'll betcha I can catch more than you, too, Grampa."

"Well, I don't think it would be a fair bet with you using those hot new lures," Hank replied with a smile.

"I'll let you borrow one and then we'll be all even."

"OK, in that case I guess we have a bet, young fella."

They stopped briefly at the bait store for a bucket of minnows then found an empty spot near the end of the fishing pier. Hank rigged Chip's line with a small hook and secured a float four feet above the hook and said, "You have awful heavy line on your reel, Chip. What pound test is this?"

"I put on thirty pound line so I wouldn't lose any of my new lures if they got snagged," Chip answered.

Hank smiled at Chip's answer and showed him how to fasten the minnow to keep it alive on the hook and they were all set.

The fall afternoon sun was pleasantly warm with low humidity produced by the arrival of a cool front the day before. The old maxim that bass fishing is never good immediately following a cold front did not hold true. When Chip's float bobbed underwater, he set the hook and reeled in a feisty twelve inch largemouth. While Hank was netting Chip's fish his own rod bent and his float went under. Hank reeled in and landed an identical schoolmate to Chip's bass.

Over the next two hours they each caught and released six small to medium size largemouth and Chip won the day with a seventeen-inch three pounder. Hank used his cell phone and snapped a picture of his grandson proudly displaying the fish before they released it back into the lake.

Helen was sitting outside reading the latest *Heritage Series* novel when she looked up and saw them approaching the Bounder. "Well, how did it go today, guys?" she asked.

"Great!" Chip exclaimed. "I caught the biggest fish today. It was way bigger than Grampa's."

"It was a really nice fish," Hank added. "I took a picture of Chip holding it with my cell phone. We'll have to email it to Ali and Preston. There's just one thing I can't understand though."

"And what would that be?" Helen asked.

"Ali always out-fished me and now it looks like she passed the baton to Chip," Hank replied.

"It's passed down in the mitochondrial DNA, sweetheart. Must come from my side," Helen joked.

That evening, Hank showed Chip how to start a campfire in the fire ring and the three of them enjoyed toasting marshmallows and making s'mores. As always happens around a campfire the conversation turned towards stories of night creatures and woods monsters. With quite a bit of embellishment, Hank told the story of his encounter, as a boy of about Chip's age, with a huge, dark, foul-smelling creature in this very campground.

"I was tent camping with my dad and my cousin, Bert, back in the primitive area when it happened," Hank related. "One night near midnight I was lying awake when I heard a noise outside the tent like someone or something had kicked one of our pans. I could see that my dad and Bert were sound asleep so I decided to take my flashlight and peek out of the tent. I stuck my head out and that's when I got a whiff of a real nasty odor, like rotten eggs. I flicked on the flashlight and it illuminated a big hairy thing that looked like it was half-man and half-gorilla. It was bent over and it looked like it was rummaging through our stuff. I was frightened like I've never been before and shouted for my dad. As soon as it heard me shout it turned and looked at me with its big shiny eyes. I was scared stiff, frozen in place, hoping it wouldn't attack us, when it just rose up on two feet, turned, and took off running upright back into the woods."

"What happened next, Grampa?" Chip asked excitedly.

"My dad and Bert woke up when they heard me holler and I told them what I had just seen. My dad tried to tell me that it was probably a black bear, but I insisted that it ran off real fast on two feet. He then tried to say it was probably a man wearing a dark colored coat and I said that it had big shiny animal eyes when it looked at me. My dad couldn't come up with any more explanations so he told us to go back to sleep. I laid awake another hour but finally drifted off to sleep."

"Did it come back again that night, Grampa?"

"Not that I know of because I eventually fell asleep, but when we got up in the morning we saw huge footprints in the dirt with a set of them leading right by our tent."

"Do you think it might still be around?"

"Well, I have heard some stories over the years that deer hunters have seen a beast like I saw and they called it a Bigfoot. In fact, a few years ago a hunter claimed that one walked right past his deer stand."

"Why didn't he shoot it!?"

"He said that he was just too scared to do anything. Besides, it looked too human to shoot. He didn't want to take a chance on facing a murder charge."

"Grampa, do you think we'll be safe here tonight?"

Helen shot Hank a look. Hank shrugged innocently.

"We'll be just fine, Chip. You don't have to be afraid sleeping inside our big motorhome."

Hank showed Chip how to douse the campfire and the three of them retired to bed safe and sound inside the Bounder. Chip seemed brave enough to sleep by himself on the sofa bed in the living area, but the morning found him between Hank and Helen in their king-sized bed.

Hank promised Helen that he wouldn't tell any more campfire monster stories.

After Helen cooked them a sausage and pancake breakfast, Hank and Chip walked the short distance to the state park marina. Chip's eye was drawn to a Yamaha trail bike parked next to the ranger's station. "I can't wait till I'm old enough to ride a bike like that," he said excitedly.

"Your mother started riding one when she was twelve," Hank responded.

"Wow! Maybe she'll let me ride one when I'm twelve, too."

Before setting out in their rental canoe, they were met by a tall light brown haired man in a park ranger's uniform. Hank noted the ranger's nametag.

"Good morning, Ranger Murray," Hank said as he held the canoe steady for Chip to board.

"Good morning," Murray said, and then proceeded to give them explicit instructions about not throwing any trash or anything else into the lake other than their fishing lines. Hank assured Ranger Murray that his lake would be safe.

"Make sure to keep that life jacket on the boy," Murray said as Hank pushed the canoe away from the dock.

"Will do," Hank replied.

As Hank was paddling away from the dock Chip said, "Boy, he was a grump."

"He's just tired of boaters throwing their trash into the water," Hank replied. "This is a beautiful lake and he just wants to keep it that way."

Their plan was to stay just off shore and toss their lures toward the banks where Hank knew there were steep drop-offs into deeper water. He figured the bass would be schooling along the drop-offs in reaction to the recent cold front. The strategy met with great success as they each landed a number of medium-sized largemouths.

Hank was pleased by how Chip's interest remained in high gear with no complaints of boredom.

"Grampa, when are we going to get to your secret spot where you used to take Mom fishing?" Chip asked.

"We're almost there. It's just up ahead and around the bend in the next cove."

"Great, I'll help you paddle there," Chip responded.

Hank watched as Chip picked up the paddle and deftly began paddling from the front of the canoe. "Where did you learn to paddle so well, Chip? Hank asked.

"We were taught how to do it in the Cub Scout summer camp. Me and a friend I met there named Jimmy won the canoe race. Next year we're joining the Boy Scouts together."

With the two of them paddling they soon rounded the corner into the cove. Hank occasionally controlled the drift as they fished, making sure not to get too close to shore. They were having limited success when Hank spotted a fallen tree across the cove. "Let's paddle over to that tree," Hank said, pointing across the cove. "I bet there's a big bass lurking near its branches. We'll fish there for a while and then head back to camp for lunch."

Hank was one up on the number of fish caught so he let Chip try his luck near the tree. "Just be careful and don't cast too far, Chip. You wouldn't want to get tangled in the tree and lose one of your new lures," Hank instructed.

Hank positioned the canoe to the right of the fallen tree and within casting distance for Chip considering the heavy line he had wound onto his reel. Chip deftly cast his lure near the bank and slowly worked it back toward the canoe. Halfway into the presentation Chip's rod bent violently as his lure was struck. He hung on with all his might as a giant largemouth catapulted from the water and tried desperately to shake the lure from its mouth.

"That's at least an eight pounder, Chip! Just keep pressure on it and don't give it any slack!" Hank instructed as Chip battled the huge fish.

Chip's arms were just about to give out when the large bass finally tired alongside the canoe. Hank netted the prized fish and carefully removed the barbed lure from its gaping mouth. He showed Chip how to grab it by its lower lip in order to hold it up while he took a picture. They both admired the lunker and weighed it before carefully releasing the eight and a half pound fish back into the lake.

"Let's try on the other side of the tree, Grampa. I'll bet there's a ten pounder over there!"

"OK, we'll try that and then we have to head back," Hank answered. "Your Gramma should have lunch ready soon."

"I can't wait to tell her about my fish!" Chip answered still highly excited about his catch.

Hank paddled the canoe to the far side of the tree and turned it broadside to the shore so Chip could make another cast with his lucky lure. Chip's cast landed close to shore but right next to a large branch of the fallen tree. He let the lure sink for a count of five and started to reel in and twitch the lure. He felt a bump and set the hook hard, anticipating another lunker bass.

Something heavy was on the line, but they didn't detect the pulsation made by the fight of a live fish.

"Uh oh, Grampa, I think I'm snagged on the tree," Chip lamented.

"Let me paddle closer to the tree and see if you can work it loose, Chip," Hank suggested.

They were now positioned directly above the snag but Chip had no luck in freeing the line. He pulled up as hard as he could and felt whatever he was snagged on start to rise, but he didn't have the strength to bring it up to the surface.

"Whatever I hooked onto started to come up but I can't pull any harder. I don't want to lose that lucky lure. Can you try, Grampa?" Chip asked as he handed the rod to Hank.

As they both watched over the side of the canoe for a telltale sign of the snagged lure Hank pulled up hard with the rod and felt the object start to rise. They could see the sparkle of the shiny lure as it made its way nearer to the sunlit surface. A moment later the snagged object came into view just under the surface of the slightly murky water.

"Oh no," was Hank's only utterance as he immediately released the bail on the reel and watched the object slowly sink back into the lake.

"Did you see what I just saw, Grampa!" Chip cried out. "Was that a sleeve? I saw a hand come up just under the water. What's he doing down there? Do you think he needs help!?"

25

"I don't think he needs our help any longer, Chip," Hank replied as he let a length of line off of the reel and snipped it.

"Why did you cut the line? How am I gonna get my lucky lure back?"

"Don't worry about your lure," Hank answered. "I'll buy you a new one. I need to tie this line to a tree branch and then we need to get back to the marina to report this to Ranger Murray."

Chapter 4

"Back so soon?" asked Ranger Phil Murray warily as Hank and Chip entered the rustic ranger station and approached the counter.

"I am afraid we have some bad news, Ranger Murray." Hank lowered his voice, "My grandson here just hooked into a man's body back in a cove to the west of the marina. It's located just on the north side of the fallen tree on the west shore of the cove in about fifteen feet of water."

"A man's body? You're joking . . ."

"I am afraid not," Hank replied. "I suggest you get on the phone with the Sheriff's Department unless you want to haul it in by yourself."

"No, I surely don't want to do that," Murray replied as he punched 911 into his desk phone with a shaking hand.

Hank overheard the woman on the line. "911 operator, Claiborne Parish Sheriff's Department. How can I help you?"

"Ma'am, this is Ranger Phil Murray down at Lake Claiborne State Park. A gentleman just came in and said he found a body in the lake."

"For the record, what is the gentleman's name?" the operator asked.

Murray looked up at Hank and said, "They want to know your name."

"Can you put them on the speaker?" Hank asked.

Murray pushed the button for the phone's speaker and told Hank to go ahead.

"Hello, this is Hank Moran. I am the person who found the body. It's in about fifteen feet of water. I can show the sheriff exactly where it is but he might need a diver to bring it up."

"OK, sir, a patrol car is on its way. Please remain onsite and wait for the officer."

"Will do, ma'am."

"Ranger Murray, I am going to take my grandson back to our campsite. I should be back by the time the patrol car arrives."

Murray just nodded in consternation with a confused look on his face.

Helen was setting out a lunch of ham and cheese sandwiches and potato salad when Hank and Chip walked in the door. "Perfect timing, guys. I was just setting out lunch."

"Gramma, you'll never guess what happened!" Chip exclaimed.

"Let's see, you had a ten pound bass on the line but it got away," Helen responded.

"Nope! I caught an eight and a half pounder and Grampa took a picture of me holding it, but then I snagged my line on a dead guy's body and lost my lucky lure."

Helen looked at Hank with a questioning expression and asked, "Did you put Chip up to this?"

"I'm afraid he's not joking. He did hook into a body," Hank answered.

"Ohh, here we go again!" Helen said as she shook her head in disbelief.

"I brought Chip back to the Bounder to stay with you while I show the sheriff where we found the body," Hank said.

"What about lunch? Can't you eat first?"

"It'll have to keep. I told the ranger that I would be right back," Hank said as he headed for the door. He stopped. "On second thought I'll take half my sandwich with me and eat it on the walk back down to the marina."

"Hank, just don't get too involved with this one!" Helen urged as he went out the door.

Hank was sitting in a rocker on the rustic front porch of the marina's bait store when a white Dodge Ram 4x4 pickup truck emblazoned with the Claiborne Parish Sheriff's Department logo pulled into the lot. The officer who exited the truck was huge in height as well as girth. Hank estimated that his six foot three frame carried around at least three hundred pounds. Despite the officer's size, he walked nimbly in Hank's direction.

Hank came down from the porch and extended his hand to greet the officer. "Hank Moran. My grandson and I are the ones who discovered the body."

"Sheriff Cecil Pettibone. Are you the famous Hank Moran from down Kenner way?

"Glad to make your acquaintance, Sheriff. Yes, I'm from Kenner, but I can't really say I'm famous."

"You are the Hank Moran that rescued that Yankee senator from the river up north, aintcha?" The sheriff said "north" like "nawth" and drew out his vowels. "And the one who received that award from the president?"

"Yep, that's me."

"Seems you have a knack for pulling bodies outta water."

"Sheriff, it's a hell of a lot more gratifying to pull out live ones than dead."

"Well, Mr. Moran, why don't you show me where this unfortunate soul's body is located. I understand it's in about fifteen feet of water? Deputy Krebs has some diving experience. He's on his way and should be arriving any minute."

Ranger Murray had the state park skiff waiting at the dock when the sheriff arrived. "Hello, Phil. Nice day for a pleasant cruise on the lake," Sheriff Pettibone said with a grin.

"I have a feeling it's not going to be very pleasant, Cecil," Ranger Murray replied. "Say, I heard about the hostage situation at the courthouse Wednesday. How is Judge Harkin?"

"Oh, he's just fine. We talked old man Boucher into giving up and releasing Judge Harkins around midnight."

As the sheriff and Ranger Murray were discussing last Wednesday night's hostage situation at the courthouse, Deputy Krebs arrived with his boat in tow.

"Ahh, here's Krebs now," the sheriff said. "When he gets his boat in the water he can follow us out to the site."

Ten minutes later the two boats left the dock and motored out the inlet to the main body of the lake. Following Hank's directions, they arrived in the cove a short time later. Ranger Murray motored across the cove to the fallen tree. When Deputy Krebs' boat pulled alongside, Hank pointed out the fishing line he had tied fast to the tree. "If you dive straight down from where the line is tied you'll find the body," Hank instructed.

Deputy Krebs was a small wiry individual who was soon stripped down to his swim pants. "I'll go down and check out the situation with my mini tank first," he said as he jumped overboard with the hand held scuba gear.

Three minutes later he resurfaced and gripped the gunwale of the ranger's boat. "There's a body down there all right," he said. "It appears to be floating about halfway down with an anchor rope tied to it. If you'll just hand me that rope with the snap hook on it over there in my boat, I'll go back down and hook it to the anchor. Sheriff, you hold onto the other end and when I give it a few yanks, start pulling."

"Phil, would you be so kind as to take a few pictures of the area and the body when it comes up?" asked the sheriff as he handed Ranger Murray a small digital camera.

"Sure will, Cecil," Murray replied.

With the rope in hand, Krebs once again disappeared under the surface of Lake Claiborne. A moment later, the sheriff felt three short tugs on the rope and proceeded to pull up on the anchor, the body following behind. Krebs remained under the water to guide the body to prevent it from hanging up again in the fallen tree.

The anchor appeared first and Sheriff Pettibone reached down and hauled it onboard being careful to only touch the rope and not the anchor itself. After pulling once again, this time on the anchor rope, the body soon appeared in the murky water. Krebs reemerged and in one quick, agile motion vaulted back into his boat.

Krebs instructed, "Sheriff, hold on to the body while I put my boat shoes back on. Then we'll get the body on board my boat. It might get a little crowded in Ranger Murray's."

Hank reached down and snipped the line to Chip's bass lure, which was still caught on the sleeve of the corpse. "I better remove the lure from his sleeve so no one gets stuck while we are hauling him into the boat," Hank said. "And,

Sheriff, if you don't mind, I'll give it back to my grandson.
It's his favorite lure."

"That's fine, Mr. Moran. I won't need it for evidence
since it had nothing to do with the demise of the drowned
Mr. John Doe. Would you kindly untie the anchor rope
from the anchor? But don't touch the anchor itself. There's
a slight chance that we might be able to lift some
fingerprints from its rubber coated surface."

Krebs maneuvered his boat close to the body, which
was now free of the anchor. He put on a pair of latex gloves
and managed to lift the upper third of the body into his
boat. Then with the sheriff's help the remainder of the
corpse was rolled over the gunwale and came to rest on its
back.

Sheriff Pettibone eyed the corpse, inhaled sharply, and
with exhaled breath managed, "Well I'll be damned!"

"You know the gentleman?" Krebs asked.

"I sure do. That's Leonard Driscoll of Driscoll Furniture
over in Shreveport! Now how in hell did he manage to get
anchored over here in Lake Claiborne?"

With Mr. Driscoll's body securely onboard his boat,
Deputy Krebs motored back to the marina with Ranger
Murray following in his wake.

The Claiborne Parish Coroner, Dr. Rufus Mills, was
waiting when the two boats tied up at the dock. Upon
initial examination of Driscoll's body the coroner found a
gash on the left side of the victim's head. Dr. Mills stated
that with the severity of the wound he doubted it was an
accidental blow. "I am afraid you have a case of murder on
your hands, Cecil."

No wallet or personal items of any sort were found in
the victim's pockets. "Could be robbery and murder," Krebs
offered.

"Rufus, how long do you think he was in the water?
Pettibone asked.

"I would say only a few days," Mills answered.

"Well, I better get back to the office," Sheriff Pettibone
said. "I have to get in touch with Shreveport so they can
notify next of kin. Thanks for your help, Mr. Moran. I hope

your grandson isn't too upset over the ordeal of finding the body."

"I'm sure he'll be OK, Sheriff. He was more upset over losing his favorite lure than seeing what it was hooked into," Hank replied.

"Mr. Moran, why don't you give me a number where I can reach you in case I have further questions."

Hank gave Sheriff Pettibone his cell number and headed back to the motorhome.

Helen was sitting at the picnic table talking on the phone with Ali when Hank walked up. "Yes, Ali, I think it's best, too. We'll head back later this afternoon. We'll see you about six."

Chip's eyes lit up when Hank laid the lure on the picnic table. "You got my lure back!" Chip exclaimed. "I can't wait to show it to my friends at school."

"If you had a lighter line on your reel you might have lost it and we never would have been aware of the body," Hank said.

"Well, I put on a heavy line in case I hooked into a monster bass."

"You did make a big catch, Chip. It's too bad it wasn't a record bass."

"Ali thinks Chip has had enough fishing for one weekend and wants us to head back to Shreveport," Helen said after ending the call from Ali.

"I kinda figured that. I caught the tail end of your conversation as I walked up," Hank replied. "I guess we better pack up and get moving."

"Aw, Grampa, must we go? Chip pleaded.

"I'm afraid so, Chip. We don't want to upset your mom and dad and spoil your chances of going on future trips with us."

Hank's cell phone rang just as they were ready to pull out of the state park campground. "Hank Moran speaking."

"Hello, Mr. Moran, this is Harold Parkinson from the Western Pennsylvania Audubon Society. I have some great news for you."

"Mr. Parkinson, good to hear from you again. Are you calling about the eagle feather?"

"Yes I am, Mr. Moran. The lab has completed the tests on the feather and the DNA does not match any known raptor. I will be presenting the findings to the Audubon Headquarters next week."

"That's great, Mr. Parkinson. Will you be reporting the feather as coming from a Washington's Eagle?"

"I am afraid not. For the time being we'll just have to label it as an unknown since there is no other sample to compare it to."

"Didn't you say that Audubon had an actual specimen?"

"Yes he did, Mr. Moran, but it was apparently lost over a century and a half ago after his death. Unfortunately, no one knows whatever happened to it."

"Well, Mr. Parkinson, at least now you have a DNA record for future comparison if another specimen should one day appear."

"That's true, and we have you to thank for it, Mr. Moran. I will be sending a copy of my report to you as well."

"Thanks for the update, Mr. Parkinson, and I will be looking forward to reading your report."

"Thanks again, Mr. Moran, have a good day. Goodbye."

"That was Mr. Parkinson on the phone from the Audubon Society. He said the DNA tests on the eagle feather showed it to belong to an unknown species."

"How about that," Helen replied. "We saw our first UFE!"

"UFE?" Hank questioned.

"Sure. Unidentified Flying Eagle."

Hank just groaned.

Chip was safely returned to his home in Shreveport that same afternoon. When they arrived they gave Ali and Preston the news that Sheriff Pettibone identified the body of Leonard Driscoll, a Shreveport furniture store owner.

Preston, sole owner of his accounting business, exclaimed, "You've got to be kidding me! Driscoll Furniture is one of my best clients. I just talked with Leonard's brother, Peter, two days ago and he said Leonard's wife, Susan, had reported him missing."

"Well, thanks to Chip and his stout fishing line, that little mystery is solved," Hank said grimly.

Chip spent Saturday night with Hank and Helen in the Bounder, which was parked in their daughter's driveway. On Sunday morning they were on their way back to Kenner after promising to make it back up to Shreveport for Thanksgiving dinner.

Hank spent the next two days reading the P.I. Test Study Manual. Most of what he read was just common sense to him. The rest of the rules and procedures stated in the manual he had learned and experienced during his thirty plus years as a Kenner, Louisiana detective.

He had made arrangements to take the P.I. test on Thursday and confidently drove the sixty miles to Baton Rouge, zipped through the test, and was back home in time for an early dinner. He was told that he should hear an answer within two weeks as to the results of the test.

Two weeks to the day he was summoned to Baton Rouge for the issuance of his Louisiana P.I. license. The Moran Investigations Agency was formally in business.

Helen had second thoughts about the name of the agency. She informed Hank, "You do realize the initials of the agency are M.I.A. Based on our recent experiences, I hope neither of us winds up Missing in Action!"

Chapter 5

Detective Craig Meyers of the Shreveport Police Department had spent a total of four days in the last month investigating the murder of Leonard Driscoll. The investigation was not a high priority case since the murder took place in neighboring Claiborne Parish. Meyers assumed that since the murder occurred out of the jurisdiction of the Shreveport Police that the investigation should be conducted by Claiborne Parish Sheriff Cecil Pettibone.

Pettibone made a halfhearted attempt at investigating the murder and got relatively nowhere. He had questioned Lake Claiborne State Park Ranger Phil Murray the day after Driscoll's body was discovered but Murray claimed that he saw nothing suspicious the previous day. In fact, he claimed that he never even saw Leonard Driscoll enter the park or launch his boat. What further hampered Pettibone's investigation was the fact that Leonard Driscoll's boat and truck were discovered at his home in Shreveport the morning after his disappearance.

Detective Meyers had routinely questioned employees of Driscoll Furniture, which was owned by Leonard Driscoll and his brother, Peter. The only bit of useful information from the store's employees was the fact that Peter and Leonard had argued heatedly a few days before Leonard's disappearance.

Since the discovery of his brother's body, Peter had made a weekly appearance at the police station to check on the progress of the investigation. During one of those visits he drank a can of Sprite that was offered by Detective Meyers. The police used the fingerprints on the can to match the ones they had found on Leonard Driscoll's boat and motor. With no other leads to go on, Peter Driscoll now became the prime suspect for his brother's murder. Adding more weight to the suspicion was the fact that Peter

Driscoll was the beneficiary of a one hundred thousand dollar insurance policy on Leonard Driscoll's life.

The Wednesday before Thanksgiving, Meyers presented Judge Harlan Mays with a request for a search warrant for Peter Driscoll's house and garage. Meyers had a difficult time convincing Judge Mays to sign the warrant, but the judge finally gave in due to the weight of the fingerprint record.

Later that afternoon, Detective Meyers and Detective Andy Granger presented the search warrant to Peter's wife, Peggy, when she answered the door. Peggy immediately called Peter at the furniture store and he arrived home fifteen minutes later to find the two detectives searching his garage.

"What in hell is going on here?" Peter demanded as he approached the two detectives.

Meyers answered, "We have a warrant to search the premises for a weapon used in the murder of Leonard Driscoll."

Peter responded with great agitation, "What? Are you saying that I am suspected of killing my brother?"

"Mr. Driscoll, you are at the top of our list of suspects," Meyers answered.

Peter said, "You'll have to excuse me. I have to call my lawyer."

"You are free to do whatever you want, Mr. Driscoll, except leave town," Meyers responded.

The search of the premises turned up only one piece of evidence and that was a short section of anchor rope, which Meyers thought looked familiar. Leonard Driscoll's boat and trailer were at the vehicle compound near the police station and upon comparing the rope found in Peter Driscoll's garage to the short section that was still tied to Leonard's boat it proved to be an exact match.

Detective Meyers then drove to the Claiborne Parish Sheriff's department to compare the rope sample found in Peter Driscoll's garage to the anchor rope that was in the evidence locker, still tied to the anchor that was used to submerge Leonard Driscoll's body in Lake Claiborne. Once again, the rope was an exact match.

Thanksgiving Day

At ten o'clock in the morning on Thanksgiving Day, Shreveport Police detectives Craig Meyers and Andy Granger knocked on the door of Peter Driscoll's home. Peggy Driscoll was in the kitchen preparing a small turkey to place in the oven. She quickly washed her hands and approached the door, hoping it was her sister-in-law. Peggy had invited Susan prior to the whole misunderstanding about Peter being involved in his brother's death, and if Susan chose to show up for dinner, Peggy would know that Susan didn't buy into any of the rumors that Peter was involved with Leonard's unfortunate, untimely demise. Besides, she thought it best that Susan not spend the holiday alone. When she opened the door, however, she was dismayed to see the two detectives who had searched her house the day before."

"Yes, what is it now?" she said.

"Ma'am, we need to speak with your husband," Meyers answered.

Peggy replied, "I'm sorry but he isn't home at the moment. I sent him to the grocery store to pick up a few things for Thanksgiving dinner. He should be back any moment. If you want, you can wait inside. I'm sure by now you're familiar with the place."

"That's OK, ma'am, we'll just wait in the car."

Five minutes later, Peter Driscoll pulled into his driveway and exited his Ford Explorer. As he approached his front door he was met from behind by the two detectives.

"Mr. Driscoll, please put down the bag of groceries," Meyers requested.

Peter turned and confronted Meyers, "Why? What do you want now?"

"Please do as we say, Mr. Driscoll. Put down the bag and face the door."

Peter did as he was told and then his hands were forced behind him and secured with cuffs.

Meyers said, "Peter Driscoll, you are under arrest for the murder of Leonard Driscoll."

He was being read his rights as Peggy came to the door. "What's going on?" she asked in a fit of panic.

"They're arresting me for Leonard's murder! Call Carlton and then Preston! Have them both come to the jail as soon as possible!"

Hank and Helen were once again greeted by Chip as they pulled their Bounder motorhome into their daughter's driveway. He excitedly gave his Gramma and Grampa big hugs when they exited the motorhome. Helen said, "Chip, didn't you forget something? You're not too big to give your Gramma a kiss!"

"Sorry, Gramma," Chip answered as he gave his Gramma a kiss and another hug.

Chip started telling them all about his show and tell in school as they made their way into the house. "I told them all about how I hooked into Mr. Driscoll's body with my lucky lure. I took the lure along to show them, along with the big story that was in the newspaper. All the other kids wanted to touch the lure but I told them it was too dangerous because it is really sharp and they might get caught!"

"Chip, your mother wants you to help set the table," Preston said. "I need to talk to your Grampa."

"OK, Dad," Chip said as he ran into the kitchen.

"I'll go help Chip," Helen said. "I want to see what all those good smells are coming from Ali's kitchen. Plus, I need to find a place to set this pie down before I drop it."

Helen was carrying one of the three shoofly pies Hank had bought and tasted up in Lancaster County Pennsylvania when they toured the Amish area.

Preston was now able to talk with Hank on an urgent matter. "Hank, this morning the Shreveport police arrested Peter Driscoll for the murder of his brother," Preston said. "I talked with him along with his attorney about an hour ago at the city jail. They claim they have enough evidence to hold him, like Peter's fingerprints on Leonard's boat and motor, and a piece of matching anchor rope in Peter's garage."

"Did Peter have an explanation for the fingerprints?" Hank asked.

"He said he replaced the fuel filter in Leonard's boat motor just a few days before he went missing and he also loaned him his boat anchor because Leonard snagged his on the bottom and had to cut it loose the last time he went fishing."

"Does Peter have anything to back up his story about changing the fuel filter?

"I am afraid not," Preston answered. "He said that he discarded the old filter in the trash. He said he also paid cash for the new filter and didn't save the sales receipt."

"What about the matching anchor rope in his garage?"

"He already admitted that it was his anchor that was fastened to his brother's body."

Hank inquired, "Why is that considered important evidence?"

"The police didn't say," Preston responded.

"Does Peter have an alibi?" Hank questioned further.

"He does, but I am afraid not a good one. On the night Leonard went missing he said he was alone, working late, going over the receipts at the furniture store, and didn't get home until ten at night. The police think he had ample time to murder his brother at the lake and get back home."

"What motive do the police think Peter had for the murder?" Hank asked.

"They interviewed witnesses who said that Peter and Leonard had argued a lot recently about the financial condition of the store. The detective found out that the brothers had taken out one hundred thousand dollar life insurance policies on each other as a business arrangement."

"Well, it seems they have a case against Peter, however a weak one," Hank offered.

"Peter claims he is entirely innocent. I told him about how you recently acquired your P.I. license and he said he would like to hire you to prove his innocence. He said the police are trying to prove his guilt and he needs someone working on his side. His reasoning is that if you can prove his innocence it would save him the cost of an expensive criminal attorney and trial. He also very badly needs to get back to the store or else it will go under."

"Didn't they set bail?" Hank asked.

"That hasn't been determined yet. Because of the holiday, his arraignment is set for Monday. His attorney is his wife Peggy's nephew. He's young and fresh out of school."

"That's just great," Hank responded. "Sounds like an interesting case for me to start out on. Can he afford a P.I.?"

"He said he can afford two hundred a day for a maximum of ten days, but that must include expenses. He is anxious for you to start right away."

"I imagine he would be anxious sitting in the Shreveport jail with a green attorney," Hank responded. "I'd like to start first thing in the morning by interviewing Peter."

"Peter is presently in the city jail on Hope Street but will be moved to the Caddo Parish Correctional Center after his arraignment. He gave me power of attorney so I will handle your fees," Preston said. "Do you need an advance to start out?"

"Not at this time," Hank answered. "I'll let you know where things stand after I talk with Peter."

"Dinner's ready!" came the call from the kitchen.

Early Friday morning Hank made arrangements to visit Peter Driscoll in the Shreveport City Jail. He was glad they towed Helen's Honda behind the motorhome for the trip from Kenner to Shreveport as they'd had plans to continue up to Branson, Missouri after Thanksgiving, but that trip would have to be delayed. It would have been cumbersome to drive the large motorhome into the city and to find a parking spot large enough for it.

Hank arrived at the Shreveport Police Department well ahead of his 10 a.m. visitation appointment at the jail to give him time to talk to Craig Meyers, the lead detective on the Driscoll case. Hank had a past acquaintance with Detective Meyers during his career with the Kenner Police Department.

Meyers greeted Hank in the waiting area. "Hank Moran, good to see you again," Meyers said as they shook hands. "I heard all about your recent exploits. How the hell are you doing?"

"None the worse for wear," Hank responded. "Although this retired life is proving to be a bit more harrowing than working for the force."

"Well, what new adventure brings you up to Shreveport?

"I've been asked to look into the Leonard Driscoll case by his brother, Peter."

"I see. I understand it was you and your grandson who discovered the body. In what capacity are you entering the case?" Meyers asked.

"I recently acquired my P.I. license and Peter wants me to help prove his innocence. I was hoping you would fill me in on what exactly you have on him."

Meyers thought a moment then said, "Our charges will be brought before the judge on Monday morning during his arraignment. I can only tell you what public knowledge is until then. We have his prints on the boat motor, matching anchor rope found in his garage, a large insurance policy on his brother, and various witnesses to testify that he recently had heated arguments with the deceased."

"I see," Hank responded. "Why is the matching anchor rope significant when he said he loaned the anchor and rope to Leonard?"

"Maybe he didn't loan it to him," Meyers replied.

"Whatever happened to Leonard's boat? Hank asked.

"Right now it is covered up out back in the compound in order to preserve the evidence. The morning after his disappearance his boat was found by his wife parked in a small empty lot just down the block from his house. It had a for sale sign on it. His truck was parked on the street by the house."

"That's strange," Hank responded. "Did you canvass the neighborhood to see if anyone had noticed whether or not the boat was there all day Wednesday?"

"That is a work in progress, Hank."

"Hmm, either he made it back home that evening and went back, or was taken back, either dead or alive, to the lake, or was killed that evening while on the lake and someone delivered the boat back to his neighborhood."

"He may have never gone fishing," Meyers responded. "The park ranger claims he didn't see Leonard Driscoll at the lake that afternoon or evening. According to Google Maps there is a fire trail that leads out to the point where you and your grandson found the body. We think Peter Driscoll hit him on the head, tied the anchor to him, and dumped him in the water. He could have done it either by land or by sea."

"Did you find anything in the boat that could have been used to strike Leonard?" Hank asked.

No, the only things left in the boat were two fishing rods, a cooler, and a tackle box."

"What was the actual cause of death?" Hank questioned further.

"The medical examiner claimed he drowned. He was still alive but unconscious when he was dumped into the lake. Not a pleasant way to go."

"Craig, you know it was just dumb luck that my grandson and I discovered Driscoll's body in the lake. What if someone wanted to divert the attention that his disappearance would generate away from the lake by relocating his rig back to his house? You would be searching around Shreveport for the answer instead of Lake Claiborne."

"But, Hank, don't you see that finding the rig in the neighborhood the night of Leonard's disappearance would help with Peter's alibi? He claimed he was working until ten o'clock that night. It would suggest Leonard made it back home alive later that evening after Peter was conveniently at home and in bed with his wife."

"I see what you mean. That is a possibility," Hank answered. "But I have a gut feeling that the answer to the puzzle lies over in Claiborne Parish and not here in Shreveport. Well, Craig, I have a ten o'clock visitation time at the jail to interview Peter and I don't want to be late. It's been good talking with you again and thanks for the information."

"You're welcome, Hank," Meyers answered. "I think you are wasting your time getting involved with this. We do believe we have the right man in custody."

"We'll see," Hank answered.

Hank left the police station and walked the short distance back to the city jail. He was searched for weapons then was seated at one of the visitation tables while a guard went back to the cell area for Peter Driscoll.

Five minutes later, the guard reappeared escorting a slim man with dark brown hair. Hank estimated he weighed about a hundred and seventy pounds in a five foot ten frame. The man looked questioningly at Hank.

"Peter Driscoll, I presume? I'm Hank Moran."

The man's face immediately lit up. He said, "I'm Peter. Thanks for coming, Mr. Moran! Has Preston told you what I need you to do?"

"Yes, he has, and please call me Hank. But before I agree to the terms he laid out, I need to hear the whole story from you, Peter. Then, if I feel you are being truthful with me, we are good to go."

"Well, to start off, I did not murder my brother like the police claim I did. They came to my house Thursday morning and arrested me. On Thanksgiving no less. They said they found my fingerprints on Leonard's boat and motor and when they searched my house and garage the day before they came up with a ten foot piece of anchor rope. I tried to tell them that I changed the fuel filter in Leonard's outboard motor two days before and loaned him my anchor to go fishing."

"Your brother's body was found over a month ago. Why did it take all this time to arrest you based mainly on your fingerprints?" Hank asked.

"I checked with the police every few days after my brother was found and they were getting nowhere in the case. I think they were frustrated and under pressure to make an arrest so they picked on me."

"I just came from Detective Meyer's office and he said you and Leonard argued lately. He said he has witnesses to substantiate the arguments."

"Hank, my brother and I have argued with each other ever since we could remember. I am sure the arguments that the detective mentioned happened at the store. Anybody who works there knows we argued all the time. It was just our way of communicating. Hell, we even argued about the best bait to use when we went fishing together and the two of us always came back alive."

Hank smiled thinking about his similar relationship with his older brother, Harold. "What about the hundred thousand dollar life insurance policy you have on Leonard?"

"That was something we did for each other to cover the final expenses so our families wouldn't be burdened if anything ever happened to one of us. Besides, the policies could be written off as a business expense. We were each other's beneficiary on the policies."

Hank studied Peter for a moment. "OK, Peter, I do believe you are being truthful with me. I will look into the case for you. First off, we need to establish an alibi for your whereabouts the night Leonard went missing. I believe that was Wednesday the twentieth of October. Preston mentioned that you were working late at the store. Did anyone see you there?"

"No, like I said, I was alone."

"What about when you left the store, did you stop anywhere?"

"No, I went straight home. I arrived there at about 10:20."

"Did you call anybody while you were at the store that evening? Your wife maybe?"

"No, I made no calls, but I did receive a call from Leonard on my cell phone," Peter replied.

"What time was that call?" Hank asked.

"It was just after five. He said he forgot to arrange for a Thursday delivery of a living room suite for Mr. and Mrs. Jorgensen. I told him I would take care of it."

"Hmm, that means Leonard was still alive at five o'clock. Did you tell Detective Meyers about the phone call?"

"Yes, I did. He said he would check the cell phone records to verify the call."

"Well, unfortunately that call does nothing to aid your alibi," Hank lamented. "However, we should be able to substantiate your story about the fuel filter. Where did you buy it?"

"I bought it at Parker Marine the Saturday before and installed it in Leonard's outboard on Monday evening."

"I understand that you threw away the receipt, but Parker Marine should still have a record of the sale."

"That's right! They did write one up."

"OK, Peter, I'll head over there as soon as we're done here. Now, do you know of anyone who might have had reason to harm your brother?"

"I can think of no one that would resort to killing him."

"Do you know of anyone that greatly disliked him?

Peter thought a moment then said, "The only person I can think of is George Hart. He is the owner of Hart Furniture, our biggest competitor. We are both struggling to keep our businesses solvent and we've had some competitive sales lately. He gets mad when we undersell him. His overhead is greater than ours so he has trouble competing. He called Leonard recently to complain that we were trying to drive him out of business. Leonard told him that he didn't need any help from Driscoll Furniture as he was doing a good job of driving himself out of business."

"Well there might be something there. I'll have to pay Mr. Hart a visit," Hank said. "Now, had Leonard been acting strange or differently in the time leading up to his disappearance?"

"Yes, he was acting edgier than usual," Peter answered. "I tried to talk to him about it but he shrugged it off saying he was just worried about the store. I heard that he was gambling recently, too, at one of the casinos. I think it was Diamond Jacks. He wouldn't talk about that either. I know he likes to play poker."

"Do you know if he had any big gambling losses?" Hank asked.

"Not that I could tell. The books at the store seem on the up and up. I wouldn't know about his personal finances though."

"If it is all right with you I'll have Preston take a look at the store's books," Hank offered. "With so little to go on, we need to do a thorough job even if it seems redundant."

"Sure, he's more than welcome to look at the books. I could have missed something."

"One more thing, Peter, Detective Meyers said that Leonard's wife found his boat the morning after his disappearance just down the street from where he lives with a for sale sign on it. Are you sure Leonard actually went fishing the day before?"

"No, I am not sure about that. I can only go by what he said on Tuesday. He said he was taking Wednesday off to go fishing."

"How is your wife coping with your arrest?" Hank asked.

"Peggy is not handling it well. She was extremely upset when the police searched our house and garage."

"I can imagine how she must feel with her house being violated like that. OK, Peter, I see the guard is pointing to his watch. Our time must be up. I'll see what I can do before your arraignment on Monday morning. Maybe we can get the charges dropped. By the way, I need to touch base with your lawyer. Do you have his number?"

"His name is Carlton Oglethorpe. He's in the phonebook."

"OK, I'll call him and let him know what I'm up to. I'll see you on Monday morning. Till then, sit tight."

"What the hell else can I do, Hank?" Peter said wryly.

Hank took the Murphy Street ramp onto I-20, crossed the Red River Bridge, and headed southeast on the Arthur Ray Teague Parkway to Parker Marine.

He entered the store, weaved his way through the numerous boats that were packed onto the showroom floor, and found the sales counter along the back wall. There he was greeted by a short, red-haired sales girl who asked if he needed help.

"Yes, I do," Hank answered. "My name is Hank Moran. I'm a private investigator working for a client of mine named Peter Driscoll. He purchased a fuel filter here on

Saturday, October 16th, and it is of extreme importance that I obtain a copy of the transaction."

"Welcome to Parker Marine, Mr. Moran, my name is Sarah. I heard about Mr. Driscoll. He was arrested for the murder of his brother. Both of them do business here. Doesn't Mr. Driscoll have his sales receipt?"

"I am afraid he threw it in the trash, ma'am."

"Well then, I'll see if I can find our copy. You said he purchased it on October 16th?

"Yes, ma'am," Hank answered.

Hank strolled around the boat showroom as Sarah searched the files back in the business office. Five minutes later she reappeared. "I found it, Mr. Moran, and I made a copy for you."

Hank perused the sales slip dated October 16th and noted Peter Driscoll's name at the top. Below his name was the price of $26.95 for a 90hp Mercury fuel filter kit.

"Thank you very much, ma'am," Hank said. "This is exactly what I need."

"Please come back and see us, Mr. Moran. We can give you a great deal on a new boat," beckoned Sarah.

"I surely will when I'm in the market for one," Hank replied as he headed out the door.

Chapter 6

"How did your interview go with Mr. Driscoll?" Helen asked when Hank entered the motorhome.

"It went well. His arraignment is on Monday morning, and barring any new evidence I am sure the judge will release him on minimal bail or even declare that the Shreveport police have insufficient evidence to warrant a trial."

"That's good news. Preston will be glad to hear that," Helen answered.

"I made arrangements with Peter to have Preston go over the store's books just to see if anything unusual shows up. His murder could somehow be related to the store. Peter told me that Leonard had words with a Mr. George Hart, who is the owner of a competitive furniture store. We are going to pay Mr. Hart a visit tomorrow."

"If we are staying up here a few more days I think we should find an RV park to stay at," Helen said. "I hate to keep blocking Ali's driveway with the Bounder and besides we'll need to hook up to the utilities soon. Ali said that there is a nice RV park up on the west side of town called Tall Pines."

"I think you're right," Hank answered. "Why don't you make the reservations while I go talk to Preston about looking over the store's books? We'll need to stay at least another week to finish the investigation."

Chip talked his mother into letting him stay with his Gramma and Grampa for one more night at the RV Park. Ali had packed a small overnight bag for Chip and made leftover turkey sandwiches to be stored in the Bounder's refrigerator. The sandwiches were a welcome treat for lunch after setting up the motorhome at the Tall Pines RV Park, their new home for the next week.

After a light dinner of vegetable soup and a spirited game of Parcheesi, Chip quickly fell asleep on the sofabed while Hank and Helen retired to the rear bedroom.

"What all have you learned on the case so far?" Helen asked.

"Well, first off, I believed Peter Driscoll when he said that he didn't murder his brother. The only evidence that the police have is Peter's fingerprints on Leonard's boat and motor and a matching piece of anchor rope that they found in his garage. The piece matched the rope that was wrapped around Leonard's body and attached to the anchor. Peter claimed he had loaned his anchor to Leonard. He said he also replaced the fuel filter on Leonard's boat motor and that is the reason his prints were present. I stopped at the boat dealer and picked up a copy of the receipt for the fuel filter. I'll need to contact Peter's lawyer tomorrow so he can present it to the judge at Peter's arraignment on Monday morning."

"I can see how the police think they have enough evidence to hold him," Helen replied. "But a fair judge should at least grant him bail. Did Peter have anything else to offer in his defense?"

"Peter said that Leonard seemed edgier than usual lately but wouldn't talk to him about it. He also said that Leonard was frequenting one of the local casinos lately, he thinks, to play poker. That's why I want Preston to go over the store's books. At this point we don't know if Leonard really had a gambling habit and if he did, how big of one."

"Well, if there is anything amiss in the books Preston will find it," Helen offered.

"We should also check out Diamond Jack's Casino tomorrow evening," Hank said. "I noticed that you still have that cup full of quarters that you won over in Biloxi last summer. You can play the slots while I check out the poker tables and inquire about Leonard's gambling habit."

"I'm feeling lucky already!" Helen responded.

The next morning Helen arose and started the coffee maker in the kitchen. Chip heard the activity and sat up in the sofabed. "Good morning, Gramma! What's for breakfast?"

"Good morning, sweetheart," Helen responded. "Your Grampa said that he is going to make your breakfast this morning."

"Does Grampa know how to cook?"

"Of course I know how to cook," Hank said as he entered the forward cabin. "This morning we are going to have egg in the hole bread."

"How do you make that?" Chip asked.

"Well, why don't you help and I'll show you'll how it's made."

"OK, Grampa, what should I do?"

"First you need to butter one side of two pieces of bread and then cut a hole in them with that round cookie cutter."

Chip proceeded to butter and cut the bread while Hank melted a pad of butter in the fry pan.

"OK, Chip, now that the pan is ready, we put the bread in the pan like this with the butter side up. We also put the two hole pieces that were cut out into the pan. Then we crack an egg into the hole in each piece of bread."

"What next, Grampa?"

"You need to pour two glasses of orange juice while I keep an eye on the eggs so I can flip them when they're ready."

With the juice poured, Chip watched as Hank flipped all the pieces and heard the sizzle when the buttered side hit the pan. One minute later they were enjoying their egg in the hole bread with a small amount of strawberry jam spread around the edges and on the two round pieces of now toasted bread. Helen opted to make herself a western omelet while Chip and Hank devoured their breakfast.

Hank and Helen dropped Chip off at his home on the way to Hart's Furniture store. Hank received the home phone number of Leonard Driscoll from Preston as he had to call Leonard's widow to arrange an interview for that afternoon.

Hart's Furniture was not hard to find on West 70th Street in the commercial district of Shreveport. Upon entering the large warehouse-sized facility, Hank and Helen were immediately set upon by a smiling salesman wearing a rainbow-colored plaid sport coat and bright yellow necktie.

"Good morning, folks. Welcome to Hart Furniture. My name is Bryan. How can I assist you?"

"Good morning, Bryan," Hank replied. "We would like to speak with Mr. George Hart."

"Oh my!" Bryan replied. "Is something wrong?"

"No, nothing is wrong. Why do you ask?"

"Well, usually when people come in to ask for Mr. Hart, they are dissatisfied with a recent purchase," Bryan offered.

"Does this happen often?" Helen asked, amused.

"Oh no!" Bryan responded. "We sell only the top grade of furniture and our customers are extremely satisfied. I thought you just might be a rare customer who found something wrong."

"I see," Helen said, not fully believing the salesman. "Would you please direct us to Mr. Hart? We would like to talk with him about a somewhat personal type matter."

"Of course," Bryan replied. "I will go and see if he is available."

When Bryan left to go to check on Mr. Hart's availability Helen said quietly, "Nice coat and tie."

"I didn't know they were hiring clowns to sell furniture now," Hank replied. "You usually see outfits like that on late night used car commercials."

"Maybe he was a used car salesman and stepped up in credibility to the furniture business," Helen offered.

"Apparently it was not too big of a step up if he is allowed to wear that jacket," Hank replied with a chuckle.

After a few minutes of browsing through the living room furniture section they spied Bryan approaching with a short stout bald man wearing an ill-fitted navy blue blazer and gray slacks.

"Mr. Hart, these are the people who would like to have a word with you," Bryan said.

"Mr. Hart, I am Hank Moran and this is my wife, Helen," Hank said as he shook Hart's hand. "I am a private investigator working on behalf of Peter Driscoll, and if you don't mind we would like to ask you a few questions in private."

51

"I saw in the paper that they arrested Peter for his brother's murder," Hart replied. "What does this have to do with me?"

"Hopefully nothing, Mr. Hart. Can we talk in your office?"

Hart led the way through aisleways crowded with unsold furniture to a small office at the rear of the store. He took a seat behind an old wooden desk that was strewn with layers of paperwork with the edges of some papers on the bottom layer beginning to yellow. "So much for a filing system," Helen muttered to Hank under her breath.

Gesturing for the Morans to be seated on two wooden chairs facing the desk he said, "Now, why would you want to question me in relation to the Driscolls?"

"Mr. Hart, we understand that your store and Driscoll Furniture are the two largest furniture stores in the area, and that there has been some heated competition lately," Hank began.

"That is true, Mr. Moran. With the downturn in the economy we have had to take every advantage possible to increase traffic to our stores."

"Peter Driscoll stated that you and his brother, Leonard, had a heated phone conversation two days before Leonard's disappearance. He also said that you were extremely angry and accused Leonard of trying to drive you out of business. Do you recall the conversation, Mr. Hart?"

"Yes, I recall the conversation," Hart replied. "I sense from your line of questioning that you may think I had something to do with Leonard Driscoll's murder and I take great offense to the insinuation."

"Mr. Hart, during a murder investigation there is initially a wide pool of suspects. An investigator's job is to narrow down that pool until the murderer is found. Now if you can convince me that you were nowhere near Lake Claiborne on the night of October twentieth we will gladly scratch your name off the list."

"Hart Furniture held an invitation only sale for our best customers on the evening of the twentieth of October," Hart answered. "The sale was quite a success and after the store closed at nine-o'clock, I treated my sales associates to a cocktail at Brady's Pub just down the street. My wife will be able to verify that I arrived home approximately at ten thirty and remained there."

"Thank you very much for your time, Mr. Hart." Hank said. "I would like to leave one of my cards with you. If you happen to think of anything that would help in our investigation, please do not hesitate to call."

"So, can I now assume that my name is crossed off of the list of suspects?" Hart asked.

"I think you may safely assume that at this point, Mr. Hart," Hank replied. "That is all for now. Thank you for your time."

As the Morans were winding their way up the aisles to the front door they were met by Bryan in the rainbow coat. "Have a nice day, folks," he said.

"Oh, Bryan, will you be having any more special invitation only sales like you had this past October twentieth?" Helen asked.

"That sale was a great success, but we only have a sale like that once a year. I'll be glad to take your name and address and send you an invitation for next year's sale," Bryan replied.

Helen handed one of the agency's cards to Bryan and said, "You may use this address. We may be in the market for office furniture in the near future."

"Thank you, Mrs. Moran. I'll keep it on file," Bryan responded.

"Well, I think Mr. George Hart has a solid alibi," Hank said as they drove back to the Tall Pines RV Park. "By the way, I liked the way you were able to verify that there actually was a big sale at the store on the night in question."

"We women have our ways to get the information we need," Helen responded.

"In that case, you better come along for the interview with Mrs. Susan Driscoll this afternoon."

While Helen was preparing lunch back at their motorhome, Hank placed a call to Mrs. Driscoll to arrange for an interview at 2:00 pm. She seemed reluctant to be interviewed at first, but Hank was able to convince her not to sit by and let her brother-in-law go to jail for a crime he did not commit. Hank thought that Mrs. Driscoll seemed to think that Peter might actually be guilty.

Hank's next call was to Peter's attorney, Carlton Oglethorpe, who answered on the second ring, "Oglethorpe Law Office. Carlton Oglethorpe speaking."

"Mr. Oglethorpe, this is Hank Moran. I need to speak with you in regards to Peter Driscoll. I am a private investigator and I am working on behalf of Peter to prove his innocence. I have some information that you will need for Peter's arraignment on Monday morning."

"I am confused, Mr. Moran. How is it that Peter hired a private detective and didn't consult with me?"

"Let's just say that I am a friend of the family, Mr. Oglethorpe."

"I see. What sort of information do you have, Mr. Moran?

"If you are familiar with his case, the charges against him are based mostly on his fingerprints being found on his brother's outboard motor. He claims his fingerprints were left on the motor from his changing of the fuel filter."

"Yes, I am aware of his claim, Mr. Moran."

"I have a copy of the purchase receipt for the fuel filter, which will help to substantiate his claim."

"That will surely help, Mr. Moran, but how do we know that he actually changed the filter?"

"I hope to get that information this afternoon when I have a talk with Leonard Driscoll's widow."

"Well, Mr. Moran, Peter's arraignment is at ten a.m. in courtroom number three. Why don't we meet there at nine-thirty to go over what you have?"

"I will meet you there, Mr. Oglethorpe."

Susan Driscoll lived in an upper middle class neighborhood in south Shreveport. Approaching Driscolls' house, the Morans passed by the empty lot where Leonard had placed his boat for sale.

"Hmm, that lot is visible from at least six houses in the neighborhood," Helen said.

"I know what you're thinking," Hank replied. "We should canvass the neighborhood to find out if Leonard actually moved the boat on the day he supposedly went fishing."

"You got it, big boy," Helen responded.

Susan Driscoll answered the door wearing a bright lime green pantsuit and matching sandals. "You must be Detective Moran," she said with a generous smile.

I guess the mourning period is over, Helen thought while taking in Susan Driscoll's outfit and smile.

"Yes, I am Hank Moran and this is my wife and associate, Helen Moran."

Wow, I think I just got a promotion to Associate Detective! Helen thought with a grin on her face.

"Please come in and have a seat. Would you join me in a cup of coffee?" Mrs. Driscoll inquired as they entered the spacious living room. "I just brewed a fresh pot."

"That would be great, Mrs. Driscoll," Hank said as he and Helen were directed to a seat on an overstuffed leather sofa.

A minute later, Susan Driscoll returned from the kitchen carrying a tray with an ornate coffee pot, three cups, a small cream pitcher, and sugar bowl.

"Please, help yourselves," she said as she placed the tray on the coffee table and took a seat in a wing chair opposite the Morans.

Hank did the honors and poured the coffee into the three cups and said, "Before we start with some questions, Mrs. Driscoll, I want you to know how sorry we are for your loss. I also know Peter is finding it difficult to cope with the loss of his brother, especially now that the police think he is the main suspect for Leonard's murder."

"I hate to think that Peter could have done something like that, but the police are certain that Peter is guilty," Mrs. Driscoll said.

"I have every reason to believe that Peter is innocent and my job is to prove it, Mrs. Driscoll. That is why we are here to ask some important questions."

"Well, Mr. Moran, what is it you need to know?

"On the Monday evening before your husband disappeared, did Peter come to your house to install a new fuel filter on Leonard's boat motor?"

"Yes, Peter did pay us a visit, and he and Leonard did work on the boat out in the driveway," Mrs. Driscoll answered.

"Did you hear either Leonard or Peter mention the fuel filter?"

"Yes, I am sure Leonard said that Peter was coming over to install a new fuel filter. It needed to be done before Wednesday so that Leonard could go fishing."

"How did Peter and Leonard get along during the installation of the fuel filter?"

"They seemed to be getting along just fine. I even heard some laughter and they each had a beer or two. Leonard was fearful that Peter wanted to give up and close the store, but I guess they worked things out."

"Do you know if Leonard also borrowed a boat anchor from Peter?"

"Yes, he did. Leonard complained that his got hung up on a snag last month over in Lake Claiborne and he had to cut the rope. I heard Leonard thank Peter for remembering to bring his anchor along."

"Very good, Mrs. Driscoll, now do you know for sure that Leonard took his boat with him when he left on Wednesday?"

Mrs. Driscoll pondered the question then answered. "Well, he said he was taking it, but it was down the street in the empty lot. I guess I didn't actually see him take the boat."

"Did you see or hear Leonard or anyone return his boat and truck that Wednesday evening or early Thursday morning?"

"No, I neither saw nor heard anyone," Mrs. Driscoll replied. "If Leonard had brought the truck home he would have parked it in our driveway and not on the street."

Hank noticed that Mrs. Driscoll seemed uncomfortable answering his questions concerning the boat. After a brief pause he continued the questioning, "Do you know of anyone who would have wished your husband any harm?"

"The police detective asked the same question. I told him no at the time and I haven't thought of anyone since then."

"Mrs. Driscoll, had Leonard been acting strangely, or should I say differently, in the time leading up to his disappearance?"

Mrs. Driscoll again pondered the question and then answered, "Yes, he seemed on edge the last month or so. He seemed short with me and didn't communicate as usual. I thought it was because of the store's financial problems."

"Peter mentioned that Leonard liked to play poker and had of late been frequenting one of the local casinos. To your knowledge, did Leonard have a gambling problem or owe any large sums of money due to his gambling?"

"I know he liked to play poker at the casino, but he always came home happy and he never gave me the impression that he lost any large amounts of money. In fact, I handle our personal finances and I would have been aware of it."

"Mrs. Driscoll, I see a picture of Leonard on your fireplace mantle. Would you mind if I take a snapshot of it with my cell phone? His picture might aid in our investigation."

"Please be my guest, Mr. Moran."

Hank rose and snapped the needed picture and said, "Thank you for being so kind to answer our questions, Mrs. Driscoll. Here is one of my cards. If you think of anything at all that would be pertinent to our investigation, please don't hesitate to call."

"I will do that, Mr. Moran, and I sincerely hope you will prove Peter's innocence."

"Do you want to canvass the neighborhood now?" Helen asked as they sat in the Honda following the questioning of Mrs. Driscoll.

"No time like the present," Hank replied. "I'll park down the street across from the empty lot. I'll take the houses on either side of the lot and you take the ones directly across the street from it."

"Am I allowed to ask questions since I don't have the P.I. license?" Helen asked.

"Just introduce yourself as an associate of the Moran Investigations Agency," Hank answered.

Hank parked in an available space across from the empty lot. "OK, let's do it. Don't forget to take your note pad, pardner," Hank said as he exited the Honda.

No one was home at the first house Hank tried. He walked down the sidewalk to the quaint two-story house on the opposite side of the lot and knocked on the door. A twenty-something woman in a blue housedress and apron answered the door. "Good afternoon, ma'am, my name is Hank Moran and I would like to ask you a few questions about Mr. Driscoll's boat that he kept on the empty lot next door."

"Are you with the police?" she queried.

"No, ma'am, I am a private investigator," Hank answered as he showed his badge. "I am working on behalf of Peter Driscoll."

"Oh, I see. Wasn't he arrested for his brother's murder?"

"Yes he was, ma'am, but we strongly believe that the police have the wrong man in custody."

"Well, I don't know if I can help, but I'll try. What is it you need to know?" she asked as a toddler appeared by her side and begged to be picked up.

"I see that you're busy," Hank said, eyeing the toddler. "I just have a few questions, so I'll be quick. As you probably know Leonard Driscoll disappeared on Wednesday, October the twentieth. Did you happen to notice if he hitched up his boat to go fishing that afternoon?"

"Yes, I sure did. I remember it because it was my husband's birthday and I had to run to the store to buy more candles for his cake. We gave him a surprise thirtieth birthday party that evening. When I went out to the car, Mr. Driscoll was in his truck backing it up to the boat. I waved to him and left. When I returned, the boat was gone."

Hank then asked, "Do you remember what time it was when you saw Mr. Driscoll with his boat?"

"Yes, it was just after twelve noon. The noon news had just come on and I turned the TV off to run to the store."

"Thank you, ma'am, you've been a great help. Can I have your name just in case this information is needed in court?"

"Yes, I'm Betty Wade."

Hank wrote her name in his notebook beside the house number he had previously recorded. "By the way, ma'am, have the police been around asking the same question?"

"No, they haven't been around," she answered

"Thanks again, Mrs. Wade, and have a nice day."

Across the street, Helen had no luck at the first two houses. One old man thought she was an Avon lady and she was told that his wife died eight years ago and he didn't need anything. After explaining that she wasn't an Avon lady, she managed to question him about the boat.

"That was over a month ago," he exclaimed. "How am I supposed to remember that? Heck, I don't even remember what I had for breakfast this morning!"

"Thank you for your time," Helen said as she turned to go.

"Wheaties!" the man suddenly shouted. "I had Wheaties for breakfast!" he added triumphantly with a big grin.

"Good for you, sir, and have a nice day," Helen replied trying to muffle her laughter.

Next door to the old man's house, an elderly gray-haired lady wearing an aqua sweat suit with a floral design answered the door after Helen saw the curtain move in what must have been an adjacent room.

"Yes, what is it young lady?" she asked before Helen had a chance to greet her.

Helen saw the sparkle in the elderly lady's eyes and thought, *I bet she knows something.* "Hello, ma'am, my name is Helen Moran and I am assisting my husband, Hank Moran. He is a private detective and is investigating the murder of Mr. Driscoll."

"Oh my, a private detective, won't you please come in, dearie? I think it is terrible what one brother can do to another. Just like Cain and Abel."

"If you are referring to Peter Driscoll as a suspect in his brother's murder, we are certain that Peter didn't do it. We are working on behalf of Peter to prove his innocence," Helen explained. "I need to ask a few questions about Leonard Driscoll's boat that he kept across the street in the empty lot."

"Why don't you come on in and have a seat," the lady beckoned.

Helen entered the house and stepped into a small foyer that led directly into the living room. She noticed a collection of colorful pottery displayed on shelves lining one wall of the room.

Helen remarked, "Why, what beautiful pottery. That one piece with the magnolia blossom looks just like one that my grandma had. I always admired it."

"That is my collection of Roseville Pottery. It is all very old. I've been collecting it for forty years. All of the pieces are in mint condition and are very valuable."

"It sure is beautiful," Helen answered. "I don't want to take up too much of your time so I'll get back to the reason we are in the neighborhood and that is to ask about Mr. Driscoll's boat."

"Well, go ahead young lady, shoot. And please have a seat."

"Please, call me Helen," Helen requested. "And your name is?"

"My name is Mildred Hardwick, but please call me Millie."

Millie sat in an old fashioned wood rocker and Helen sat on a yellow wingback chair facing her.

"Millie, Mr. Driscoll disappeared on October twentieth. He told everyone that he was going fishing that afternoon in his boat and I need to know if you saw him leave with the boat on that day."

"No, I didn't see him take the boat and I didn't remember if the boat was or wasn't on the lot that afternoon, but I did hear something strange during the night and I noticed something unusual about the boat the next morning."

"What did you hear during the night, Millie?" Helen asked trying to hold back the excitement.

"I'm on two different blood pressure medicines and it is a rare night that I don't have to haul my old butt out of bed and take a trip to the bathroom in the middle of the night to relieve myself. After doing my business in the bathroom I was on my way back to bed when I heard some truck noise and some banging that sounded like it came from across the street. I looked out my front window and saw someone unhitching the boat from a truck. Then the person got into the truck and moved it up the street. Shortly after that I heard the sound of one of those whiny motorbikes start up and leave. And then everything was quiet so I went back to bed."

"Millie, were you able to recognize the person unhitching the boat?"

"I'm afraid not, dearie. It was very dark out that night. I think the person might have been wearing some kind of a uniform, but like I said, it was very dark out and I can't say for sure. I can say for sure that it was Mr. Driscoll's truck because it sounded the same."

"You said something was unusual about the boat when you saw it the next morning. What did you see?" Helen asked.

"Well, Mr. Driscoll always had the boat parked sideways on the lot so passersby could get a good look at it with the For Sale sign on it. The next morning I noticed that it was just backed into the lot like someone was in a hurry to drop it off."

"So what I guess you're saying is ... the boat was probably moved that Wednesday and brought back early Thursday morning?"

"I'm just telling you what I heard and observed, dearie. You can make your own conclusion," Millie answered.

"That's great information, Millie. Have you noticed anything else strange in the neighborhood, like a vehicle that doesn't belong or strangers lurking around the Driscolls' house?"

"No, the only person I saw lurking around the Driscolls' house was Mike Billings. He's a plumber who lives on this side of the street directly across from the Driscolls."

"What do you mean by lurking around, Millie?" Helen asked.

61

"Well, from my observation Mr. Billings and Mrs. Driscoll take turns of late occasionally visiting each other's house when Mr. Driscoll isn't around."

"Oh, do you mean they are having an affair?" Helen asked.

"I'm only telling you what I observed, dearie, and once again you can make your own conclusions."

"Thank you for all the great information Millie," Helen said as she rose from her chair.

"Won't you stay and join me in a cup of tea?" Millie asked.

"No, I can't, but thank you for asking, Millie. My husband is outside in the neighborhood and he's probably wondering where I am."

"Well, you take care, young lady, and stay out of danger, you being a private eye and all."

"I'll do that, Millie, and thanks again. Oh, here is one of my husband's cards. If you happen to think of anything else, please don't hesitate to call."

Helen came out of Millie's house and noticed Hank was waiting in the Honda. "Have any luck?" Helen asked as she entered the car.

"The neighbor next to the empty lot definitely remembered Leonard hitching up the boat to his truck that Wednesday. How did it go on your side of the street?"

"One old gentleman thought I was an Avon lady and he was very proud that he remembered that he had Wheaties for breakfast," Helen replied.

"Interesting bit of information, but I don't think it will help us solve the case," Hank said with a chuckle.

"However, the old guy's next door neighbor, Millie Hardwick, did provide something that might prove very helpful. It seems that Millie is the unofficial neighborhood watch and apparently doesn't miss much. She had to get up very early that Thursday morning to relieve her bladder and heard truck noise and some banging. She looked out the front window and saw someone she couldn't identify unhitch the boat and drive up the street. The person might have been wearing a uniform. Shortly thereafter she heard a whiny motorbike start up and leave. At daylight she noticed Leonard's boat was parked at an odd angle in the lot as if someone dropped it off in a hurry. She claimed that Leonard always positioned the boat broadside to the street so that it and the For Sale sign were readily visible."

"Hmm, the sound of the motorbike is interesting," Hank commented. "Whoever murdered Leonard and delivered his boat back to the neighborhood could have easily transported a lightweight motorbike in the truck and then used it for the trip back home. The part about the uniform is also very interesting."

"Ms. Millie was unsure about the possibility of the person wearing a uniform because of the dark night, but that's not all she had to say," Helen added. "It seems that she observed Mrs. Driscoll and the neighborhood plumber who lives across the street making frequent trips back and forth to each other's houses when Leonard wasn't around."

"Do you think he was fixing her plumbing?" Hank asked.

"In more ways than one," Helen replied. "His name is Mike Billings."

"Maybe we should pay Mr. Billings a visit," Hank suggested.

"I don't think he's at home," Helen replied. "I saw his white van in his driveway when we came out of Mrs. Driscoll's house, but it is gone now. He's probably out on a call."

"Well, we can add him to the list of suspects and talk with him later," Hank said. "Plumbers sometime wear uniforms. You didn't happen to notice a motorbike around his house, did you? He could have ridden one over to the lake and then brought it back home in the boat." Hank craned his neck to get a better view of the plumber's driveway. "His garage door has windows in it. We can take a peek to see if there's a bike in the garage."

"No, we better not. Ms. Millie might see us and alert him," Helen replied, recalling Millie's penchant for watching her neighbors' houses through her curtains.

"We can ask him if he owns one when we interview him then," Hank responded.

"Well then, we should get back to the Bounder to rest up and get ready for our big night at the casino," Helen said. "I only feel lucky when I'm reinvigorated."

Helen was excited about the investigation as they drove back to the campground. "I think I might have found a new calling. How do I become a real P.I. in the Moran Investigations Agency?"

"We'll have to check when we get back to Kenner, but I think all you have to do is apply for an apprentice license, which is good for one year. Then within that year you must complete the basic training course and pass the exam," Hank explained.

"I want to do it," Helen said matter-of-factly.

"OK," Hank said grinning and thinking about what the rest of their lives would be like as partners in a private investigation agency.

Chapter 7

Hank found the snapshot of Leonard Driscoll's photograph that he took with his cell phone, transferred it to his laptop, and made a copy on the portable printer he had procured for use in the motorhome. They were now ready for their trip to the casino, which was only a fifteen minute drive from the RV Park.

With Helen by his side, carrying her large cupful of quarters, they made their way from the concrete parking garage to the large barge made up like a riverboat that held Diamond Jack's Casino. The casino wasn't directly on the river but was moored in what could best be described as a pond adjacent to the river.

Upon traversing the elaborate gangplank they entered the casino and immediately heard the unmistakable din of hundreds of slot machines' beeps, bonks, and whistles. "Music to my ears," Helen remarked as she shook her large plastic cupful of quarters.

"I'm going to head over to the poker tables to try to question the dealers," Hank said as they paused inside the entrance. "I'll look for you at the slots when I'm done."

"Sounds like a first rate plan," Helen said as she squeezed Hank's hand and turned and headed toward the slots and their alluring clamor.

Hank walked up to the Four Card Poker table and watched as the dealer dealt out cards to the players and to himself. Hank understood that in this version, the players played against the dealer. Each player received five cards to make the best four card poker hand possible. However, he saw that the dealer received six cards to give the house the advantage.

When the hand was played out, two players beat the dealer and three lost. Before dealing the next hand the dealer said to Hank, "Good evening, sir, we have an empty chair if you care to join in on the fun."

"Thanks for asking, but I don't like the odds," Hank replied. "I was wondering if you could take a second to help me out," Hank continued as he discretely opened his coat to reveal his badge that was fastened to his belt.

The dealer nodded, which Hank interpreted as a go ahead, and so he showed the man the picture of Leonard Driscoll. "Was this gentleman a player at your table up until last month?"

"He looks kinda familiar but he didn't play at my table. You might want to ask Bernie at the Texas Holdem table."

Hank gave him a thumbs up and moved on. He found three Texas Holdem tables and noticed one a dealer with the name badge, "Bernie." Hank waited until the present hand was played out and said, "Bernie?" as he again discretely flashed his badge to the dealer and showed him the picture. "Does this gentleman look familiar to you?" Hank asked.

Bernie nodded and said, "I have a break coming up after the next hand. I'll meet you in the lounge."

Hank gave Bernie a nod and went to find Helen. He found her as she fed a quarter into a slot machine and pushed the play button. The machine did its gyrations and beeped as ten quarters dropped into the tray.

"Looks like you're having some luck," Hank said.

"I was down to about a quarter of my cupful but I won them all back so far," Helen replied

"If you can tear yourself away from the machine I would like you to accompany me to the lounge to talk to a dealer named Bernie," Hank requested.

"It's a good time to quit, now that I about broke even," Helen answered. "I'll invest a few more quarters later."

Hank found a booth in the lounge and he and Helen sat and waited for Bernie to show. A waitress approached and took their drink order. Helen ordered a glass of chardonnay and Hank got a bourbon and water.

The waitress returned with their drinks as Hank saw Bernie enter the lounge and waived at him. As he approached the booth the waitress asked, "The usual, Bernie?"

"Not just now, Alice. I already had my limit," he replied.

Bernie pulled up a chair from a table across the aisle and sat at the end of the booth. "Are you with the Shreveport P.D.?" he asked Hank.

"No, I'm private," Hank answered. "I'm working on behalf of Peter Driscoll."

"I see. I read what happened to Leonard in the newspaper. It's a shame. He was a decent guy. I can't believe his brother would murder him."

"We are sure he didn't," Hank responded.

Bernie considered Hank's answer then asked, "Well, how can I help you? I only have a few minutes."

"I appreciate you taking the time. How often did Leonard frequent your table?" Hank asked.

"Leonard came in about once a week, usually on a Friday night."

"Was he a heavy better?"

"No, not Leonard," Bernie answered. "He just enjoyed playing the game. He would have been happy playing penny ante if we had a table."

"Then he didn't suffer any heavy losses I assume?" Hank asked.

"No, not Leonard," Bernie answered again. "He usually broke about even, but he did always leave a nice tip. I think it was mainly to impress his lady friend though."

"His lady friend? What did his lady friend look like?" Hank asked.

"Well, she was brunette and much younger than him."

Helen perked up thinking that Susan Driscoll could appear younger in the dim lights of the casino and asked, "Leonard didn't by any chance call his lady friend by the name of Susan, did he?"

"No, now let me think." After a pause Bernie answered, "I think he called her Lucy."

"I see. When was the last time you saw him here at the casino?" Hank asked.

"I remember it was the Friday before I saw the newscast about his disappearance. The reason I remember it was because as Leonard and his friend were leaving he happened to pass by the slots and dropped a buck in a machine just for passing luck. The son-of-a-gun hit a ten thousand dollar jackpot."

Helen smiled, laughed, and said, "Some people have all the luck."

"Yeah, but it appears his luck ran out the next week," Hank offered.

Bernie the dealer nodded. "Well, good people, I have to get back to my table. I hope I've been of some help to y'all," he said as he rose from his chair.

"You've been a great help indeed," Hank answered as he handed Bernie one of his agency cards. "If you think of anything else that may help, please call."

"Will do," Bernie answered as he left to return to his Texas Holdem table.

"This case just keeps getting more interesting by the minute," Helen remarked.

"We can now add Ms. Lucy as another player to the game, Hank said. "I wonder if Susan Driscoll knew about her."

"If she didn't, I have a feeling she soon will," Helen answered.

"Yes, I'm afraid so," Hank responded as he finished off his bourbon. "Do you want to play some more slots before we leave?"

"No, I've had enough for one evening. Just take me home ... lover boy."

Hank raised his eyebrows mischievously.

Helen just smiled and winked.

Sunday morning was quiet at the Tall Pines RV Park. Hank made his usual trek to the campground office for the morning paper while Helen prepared a breakfast of eggs benedict. When Hank returned to the Bounder Helen announced that she just had a call from Ali and they were invited for Sunday dinner.

"That's great. We need to talk with Preston about his audit of Driscoll Furniture's books," Hank replied.

"Ali did mention that he found a few interesting entries," Helen added.

"Why don't we get ready early and swing by Mrs. Driscoll's neighborhood?" Hank suggested. "There's a good chance that Mike the plumber will be at home, being it's a Sunday."

"I guess I can save my crossword puzzle for later," Helen said. "A talk with Mike Billings might prove very interesting. We can also stop in at Susan Driscoll's afterward to ask her if she suspected that Leonard was stepping out on her."

Hank parked the Honda in front of the house next door to Susan Driscoll's and walked with Helen across the street to knock on Mike Billings' front door. Billings' white van was parked in the driveway but after repeated knocks they received no answer. They walked back across the street to Susan Driscoll's house and started up the driveway. As they approached the house a man dressed in a sweat suit and sneakers came out the door.

"I saw you across the street knocking on my door. If you are Jehovah's Witnesses forget it. I'm not interested."

"I assume you are Mike Billings?" Hank asked.

"Yeah, so what?" Billings answered. "Who are you?"

"I'm Hank Moran of Moran Investigations, and this is my wife and associate, Helen Moran. We're investigating the death of Leonard Driscoll and need to ask you a few questions."

"A private detective, huh? Why would you want to question me about Leonard's death?"

"Think back to the Wednesday that he disappeared. We just need to know if you saw Leonard Driscoll leave the lot down the street with his boat in tow."

"I don't remember the last time I saw him leave with the boat. Besides it's none of my business and I'm usually out on plumbing jobs most days."

"Mr. Billings, what is your relationship with Susan Driscoll?" Helen asked.

"Now *that* is none of *your* business," Billings answered.

"We know that you and Susan Driscoll had been seeing a lot of each other, before and after her husband's death," Helen continued prying.

"I am, or was, a friend to both Susan and Leonard," Billings answered. "And I already told you that it's none of your business."

Trying to catch Billings off guard Hank asked, "Mr. Billings, do you own a motorbike?"

69

Billings took a moment to gather himself from the sudden change in questioning and answered, "Yes, I own a trail bike. What of it?"

Just then the front door opened and Susan Driscoll appeared wearing an expensive looking house coat. "Mr. and Mrs. Moran, what are you doing here?"

"I was just leaving," Billings interrupted and turned and walked across the street to his house.

"Mrs. Driscoll, may we come in?" Hank asked. "We have uncovered some additional information about your husband and would like to talk with you further."

"Yes, please come in," she answered.

They sat in the same arrangement as they had during yesterday's interview.

"I know how this may look with Mike Billings just leaving, but he has been a great friend and I don't think I could have made it through the last few months without him. And I'm sorry I can't offer you coffee. It seems I just ran out," Susan Driscoll said.

"That's OK, Mrs. Driscoll, we won't be long," Helen said.

Susan Driscoll looked at Hank and asked, "Now what is this additional information you have about Leonard? And please, call me Susan."

"Susan, had Leonard ever mentioned anyone by the name of Lucy?" Hank asked.

Hank could tell the question hit a nerve with Susan. She seemed to feign thinking about the question then answered, "I think he did on occasion mention someone by the name of Lucy who handled some advertising work for the store. She was a commercial artist and created some newspaper spreads."

"Susan, this next question might prove difficult for you. Were you aware that a younger woman by the name of Lucy accompanied Leonard numerous times to Diamond Jack's Casino?"

The question seemed to have no shock effect at all on Susan as she took her time to formulate an answer. "Yes, I knew about his affair with Lucy Chatham."

"Did Leonard know about your affair with Mike Billings?" Helen asked.

Susan stared at the floor before she answered, "You might as well know the whole story. Yes, both Leonard and I have had extra-marital affairs, which we both found out about. We had an appointment scheduled with a marriage counselor on Friday the twenty-third, but as things turned out he never came home Wednesday night. We were going to try to reconcile our marriage."

Susan grabbed a tissue from the box beside her chair and dabbed at her eyes. However, Hank noticed no presence of tears.

"How did Mike Billings feel about your reconciliation with Leonard?" Hank asked.

"He became upset when I first told him, but then he seemed to settle down and wished me luck. He seemed sincere when he said he was glad to see his two friends try to save their marriage."

Some friend! Helen thought.

"That's all we have for now, Susan," Hank said. "We apologize for having to delve into your personal affairs, but it may prove relevant to the case."

"I'll do whatever is necessary to find my husband's murderer," Susan responded.

On the short drive to Ali's house, Hank and Helen discussed the case. "Is Mike Billings our main suspect?" Helen asked.

"He's at the top of the list for the moment," Hank answered. "He had the means and a possible motive. We also have to find out more about Ms. Lucy Chatham and see if she knew about Leonard and Susan's reconciliation plans."

"It also wouldn't hurt to find out if Susan cashed in on a large life insurance policy on Leonard," Helen said.

"You do have an inquiring mind, Mrs. Moran. I think you have the makings of a fine detective. In my career I have found that the motives in most murder cases boil down to three things."

"And what are they, sweetheart?"

"Love, hate, or money. Or any combination of the three."

Ali served a delicious meal of Cajun meatloaf, mashed potatoes, gravy, and Brussels sprouts. The meatloaf had just enough cayenne pepper and hot sauce to make the back of Hank's neck damp. The extra bottle of Tabasco Sauce on the table went unused. When Hank was stuffed to the gills he managed to ask Preston about his perusal of the Driscoll Furniture books.

"I found two interesting entries in the ledger," Preston said. "The first was the deposit of a three thousand dollar check from Hegemon's Furniture Manufacturing based up in Little Rock."

"Why is that of interest?" Helen asked.

"Usually Driscoll Furniture paid Hegemon, not the other way around," Preston explained.

"He could have borrowed money from Hegemon to meet the store's payroll," Hank suggested.

Chip, who was sitting quietly at the table spoke up and offered his explanation: "Maybe Mr. Driscoll was blackmailing Mr. Hegemon and Mr. Hegemon bumped him off so he wouldn't have to pay him any more money."

Hank chuckled at Chip's idea and said, "It looks like we have a junior detective in the family. Chip, where did you learn about blackmail?"

"I heard it on a detective show on TV and then I looked it up in the dictionary on my computer," Chip answered.

"Well, actually, Chip, your idea may not be too far-fetched," Hank said. "I ran across a similar situation when I was on the force. It wouldn't hurt to check out Mr. Hegemon."

"Preston, what was the second item that you found?" Ali asked.

"On the Monday before Leonard disappeared he made a deposit of six thousand five hundred dollars with no record of where the money came from," Preston said.

"Aha, we know where it came from," Helen said. "The Friday before, he hit a ten thousand dollar slot machine jackpot at Diamond Jack's Casino."

"I wonder what he did with the other thirty-five hundred," Hank pondered.

"Maybe he gave it to his lady friend," Helen suggested.

"Preston, were there any checks written to a person named Lucy Chatham?" Hank asked.

"Let me think ... yes, there were two checks written in the last six months. They were written under the advertising budget for just over three hundred dollars each. And what is this about Leonard having a lady friend?"

"Both Leonard and Susan Driscoll were seeing other people. They had decided to seek the help of a marriage counselor, but Leonard disappeared a few days before their scheduled appointment," Helen explained.

"So, he was stepping out with Lucy Chatham? I find it hard to believe that Leonard was the type," Preston remarked.

"Would it be possible for you to get Ms. Lucy's address and phone number?" Hank asked Preston.

"I think so. I brought Leonard's Rolodex home with me along with the ledger just in case I had to cross reference some entries. It's back in my office," Preston answered.

"Check to see if you have the information for Hegemon's Furniture Manufacturing also," Hank requested.

Preston retreated to his office and returned a short time later with a printout containing a copy of both Lucy Chatham's and Hegemon's Rolodex cards and handed it to Hank.

"This is interesting," Hank said as he looked at the printout. "Lucy Chatham lives over in Homer, which is only a few miles from Lake Claiborne."

"Hmmm, we'll also have to check if Ms. Lucy had access to a trail bike," Helen offered.

"What's the significance of a trail bike?" Preston asked.

"We have a witness who heard a small engine motorbike leave the scene the night Leonard's boat was returned to his neighborhood," Helen replied.

"Well, you two sure have dug up a lot of information in the last two days. I think Peter has done well in hiring you." Preston said.

"Thanks, we try," Hank answered.

On Monday morning, Hank entered the Caddo Parish Courthouse a half hour before Peter's arraignment to meet with Peter's lawyer, Carlton Oglethorpe. Hank recognized him immediately from the picture the young lawyer emailed to him the previous afternoon.

Oglethorpe gave the appearance of an athletic young man who looked like he would be more at home on the football field than in a courthouse. His firm handshake further enhanced Hank's impression of him.

"Good to meet you, Mr. Oglethorpe," Hank said as they shook hands.

"Likewise, Mr. Moran," Oglethorpe replied. "I had my secretary do some research into your background and I was greatly impressed with your record during your career with the Kenner P.D. and even more so with your recent exploits up in Michigan. And as long as we'll be working together on Mr. Driscoll's behalf, please just call me Carlton."

"Will do, Carlton, and please, call me Hank. Here is the copy of the receipt for the fuel filter that Peter purchased to repair his brother's boat motor. Leonard's wife did confirm that Peter changed the filter. Now, there are a few things we uncovered over the weekend that you should be aware of before the arraignment."

Oglethorpe pointed to a bench and suggested they sit so he could take notes.

"OK, Hank, what have you got?" Oglethorpe said as he pulled out his yellow legal pad from his briefcase.

"First, and most important, we have a witness who saw Leonard's boat being returned to the empty lot at about three in the morning. Immediately following this she heard a motorbike start up and leave the neighborhood."

"So, it would be impossible for Peter to be the murderer because he was at home and in bed with his wife at the time the boat was being returned," Oglethorpe surmised.

Hank smiled at Oglethorpe's quick deduction and said, "The second thing is, Leonard and his wife, Susan, were cheating on each other and had an appointment to see a marriage counselor for reconciliation the Friday after he disappeared. Susan was seeing the plumber across the street and Leonard was seeing a younger woman named Lucy Chatham, who just happens to live in Homer, about three miles from where I found his body."

"Hmm, that knowledge might help. It does throw open the possibility of additional suspects and could create more doubt in the judge's mind," Oglethorpe commented.

"OK, I see everyone is heading into the courtroom," Hank said. "Let's see if we can break Peter out of here."

Judge Harlan Mays presided over the proceedings. It must have been a low crime time period over the holiday weekend as there were only three other cases besides Peter's. Two men arrested for DUI were released on one thousand dollars bail each and one woman was arrested for spousal abuse. She apparently hit her husband over the head with a frozen Thanksgiving Day turkey because he forgot to take it out of the freezer two days before to defrost. He was presently in the hospital with a concussion. She was released on five hundred dollars bail. Hank thought it looked encouraging that Judge Mays was so liberal with granting bail requests.

The few remaining people in the courtroom were Peter Driscoll, Peggy Driscoll, Hank, Attorney Oglethorpe, District Attorney Drew Callahan, Detective Craig Meyers, and two uniformed security personnel. Judge Mays eyed the remaining people then said, "Now we get to the case of Mr. Peter Driscoll. Mr. Callahan, what are the charges?"

"The people of Caddo Parish contend that Peter Driscoll willfully murdered his brother, Leonard Driscoll, on the twentieth of October, 2010 by bludgeoning and drowning the victim in Lake Claiborne in Claiborne Parish," Callahan replied.

"How does Mr. Driscoll plead to the charges against him?" Judge Mays asked.

"I plead innocent of the charges against me, Your Honor," Peter replied."

"Your plea is so noted," said Judge Mays.

A very confident Carlton Oglethorpe spoke up, "Your Honor, I would like to enter a pre-trial motion to dismiss the case against Peter Driscoll due to lack of sufficient evidence."

"I see, young man. I assume you are Mr. Driscoll's attorney. I haven't seen you in my court before. What is your name?"

"My name is Carlton Oglethorpe, Your Honor."

"Any relation to Billy Oglethorpe?" Judge Mays asked.

"Billy Oglethorpe is my grandfather, Your Honor."

Judge Mays' face lit up with a big smile. "How is the old billy goat handling retirement?"

"He's as feisty as ever, Your Honor," Oglethorpe replied.

Judge Mays, still smiling, turned to D.A. Callahan and asked, "Mr. Callahan what is the evidence you have against Mr. Driscoll?"

"Your Honor, Peter Driscoll's fingerprints were all over his brother's boat and motor. A length of anchor rope was found in Peter's garage that matched the anchor rope that was attached to the anchor that weighed down Leonard Driscoll's body. Peter Driscoll was heard in a heated argument with his brother the week before his disappearance. Peter Driscoll was the beneficiary of a one hundred thousand dollar life insurance policy on Leonard Driscoll. And, finally, Peter Driscoll has no verifiable alibi for the time of his brother's murder."

"Hmm, on the surface, the evidence is only circumstantial but seems sufficient to send the case to the grand jury," Judge Mays commented. "What have you to say, Mr. Oglethorpe?"

"Your Honor, Private Investigator Hank Moran of the Moran Investigations Agency has been very busy over the weekend and has uncovered critical information that counters the charges against Peter Driscoll," Oglethorpe replied. "With your permission I will let Mr. Moran relate his findings."

"Mr. Moran, I am not familiar with your agency. Is your agency licensed in our state of Louisiana?" Judge Mays asked.

"Your Honor, my agency is one month old and is based in Kenner, where I was a detective with the Kenner P.D. for over thirty years," Hank replied.

"Why does your name sound so familiar to me?" Mays asked.

"Perhaps you heard my name on the national news relative to a certain event concerning a noted U.S. senator from Michigan," Hank replied.

"Ahh, yes, I remember now," Judge Mays replied. "You rescued the senator from a river up there and I believe that you were also presented a distinguished citizen's medal by the president."

"You are correct, Your Honor," Hank replied.

"Well, welcome to my courtroom, Mr. Moran. The young Mr. Oglethorpe said you were busy over the weekend. Please tell us what you found with regards to Mr. Driscoll."

"I will address each item of evidence in the order that they were presented by D.A. Callahan." The judge nodded and Hank began. "He first mentioned Peter Driscoll's fingerprints on his brother's boat and motor. Peter changed the fuel filter on his brother's boat motor the Monday before his brother disappeared. This fact was verified by Leonard's widow, Susan Driscoll. I also was able to obtain a copy of the sales receipt for the purchase of the fuel filter kit from Parker Marine." Mr. Oglethorpe walked forward and handed the receipt to Judge Mays. Hank continued, "The repair took place in Leonard Driscoll's driveway and was witnessed by Mrs. Driscoll. The repair is the reason Peter Driscoll's fingerprints were on the boat and motor."

"Next is the matter of the anchor rope," Hank continued. "Leonard Driscoll lost his boat anchor during a fishing trip to Lake Claiborne the previous month. The loss of the anchor was confirmed by Susan Driscoll. She also confirmed that her husband borrowed Peter's anchor and rope, which Peter brought with him when he repaired Leonard's motor. It was Peter's anchor that was found connected to Leonard's body and that is the reason a matching piece of anchor rope was found in Peter's garage."

Hank further stated, "Next, I will address the witnessed argument between Peter and his brother. Peter and his brother enjoyed arguing with each other. According to Peter, it was a normal occurrence to argue in an amusing manner about most anything. He claims they even argued about the best lure to use whenever they went fishing together and they both came back alive. Susan Driscoll said that both Leonard and Peter were laughing together and shared a few beers the evening Peter changed the fuel filter. This was two days before Leonard's disappearance."

Hank noticed Judge Mays taking notes and occasionally glancing towards D.A Callahan. "This is all very interesting," the judge said. "Please continue, Detective Moran."

"Driscoll Furniture was the purchaser of one hundred thousand dollar life insurance policies on Peter and Leonard," Hank continued. "The beneficiary on both policies was the surviving brother. It was a mutually agreed upon arrangement to cover their final expenses so as not to burden the families."

"Now, it is true that Peter does not have a rock solid alibi for the evening of Wednesday the twentieth of October up until about ten p.m. when he arrived at home," Hank conceded. "Peter said he was working late at the store, but as there are no security cameras from the office to the parking lot, we could not substantiate it. Peter did receive a cell phone call from Leonard at approximately five p.m. to inform him of a furniture delivery that had to be made the next day, so we do know that Leonard was still alive at that time. In the course of questioning Leonard's neighbors we found two witnesses. The first will testify that she saw Leonard Driscoll leave with his boat on Wednesday afternoon. The second witness saw a person returning Leonard's boat to the empty lot where he normally kept it at approximately three a.m. The witness also stated that the boat was not parked the way Leonard normally parked it and that she heard a small motorbike start up and leave the scene. We contend that the person who murdered Leonard Driscoll returned Leonard's boat at that time and left on a small motorbike. That person could not have been Peter Driscoll, as he was at home and in bed at the time."

"Well, Detective Moran, it seems you did a thorough job in refuting all of the Shreveport P.D.'s evidence against Mr. Driscoll. Detective Meyers, the information brought forth by Detective Moran implies that you did not do a very thorough investigation. Did you in fact question Leonard Driscoll's neighbors about the boat situation?"

"No, Your Honor, that was on our list of things to do this afternoon," Meyers replied.

"Well in my opinion that should have been done before Mr. Driscoll's arraignment," Judge Mays stated. "It is also my opinion that Mr. Peter Driscoll is free to go home. District Attorney Callahan and Detective Meyers, the next time you come into my court please have real evidence and not mere speculation as to the guilt of the accused!"

With the rap of his gavel Judge Mays declared, "Court adjourned!"

Court security removed the handcuffs from Peter and he was immediately greeted with an embrace from his wife. After releasing Peggy, Peter made his way to Hank. "Hank, I don't know how I can ever thank you enough for the fantastic job you did."

"Peter, I could not have done it without the help of my wife and partner, Mrs. Moran," Hank replied. "She found the witness who saw the boat being returned. Now, if you don't mind, we still have about a week left in our agreed upon ten day time limit. Once I start a case I like to finish it. I would like to continue the investigation into your brother's murder."

"Please take all the time you need, Hank. My name won't be entirely cleared in the public's eye until the real murderer is found."

Hank was approached by Detective Meyers in the hall outside of the courtroom. "Hank, you really did a number on us in there. We thought we had enough to hold Peter over for trial and were planning to continue the investigation. We were not counting on him hiring you."

"Where do you stand at this point?" Hank asked.

"I'll have to talk to Callahan, but other than Peter Driscoll we have no additional suspects. Since the crime occurred over in Claiborne Parish, he just might claim it falls under the jurisdiction of the Claiborne Parish Sheriff's Department."

"Craig, Peter Driscoll wants me to continue my investigation into Leonard's murder. Is there anything you might have that would help that you did not disclose?"

Craig Meyers smiled and said, "I have a photograph of a tire tread left by a small motorbike. The tread mark was found in the gutter directly behind Leonard Driscoll's truck parked on the street in front of his house. If you give me your address I can email it to you."

Hank gave Meyers his card and said, "My cell number is at the bottom. I always thought you were a stand-up guy and a gentleman, Detective Meyers."

"Good luck with your investigation, Detective Moran," Meyers said as they shook hands. "If you need any help from the Shreveport P.D. give me a call."

"I'll do that," Hank replied.

Chapter 8

Helen could tell things went well at Peter's arraignment by Hank's beaming smile as he entered the Bounder. "Looks like you have good news," Helen said.

"Peter is home free!" Hank replied. "After my presentation of our findings, Judge Mays ruled there was insufficient evidence to hold Peter over for trial. In fact, it looks like the Shreveport P.D. is dropping out of the case and leaving it up to the Claiborne Parish Sheriff's Department to solve."

"That's great!" Helen replied. "I assume we are off the case and we can head home. I'm anxious to apply for my apprentice P.I. license."

"Well, not so fast. Peter wants us to continue with our investigation. He said his name won't be entirely cleared in the public's eye until the person who murdered his brother is found. I agreed to continue. I just couldn't walk away and let things hanging. You know me, once I start something I have to finish it."

"That's fine, but if we are planning to stay up here I'm going to have to impose on Ali to let me do some laundry."

"Ahh, the necessities of life," Hank replied. "It's great to have an agency partner who can also do the laundry."

"Uh huh, well one of these days *you* are going to apply for *your* apprenticeship in *laundering*, big boy!" Helen retorted.

"Great, I can just see me wearing pink underwear," Hank replied.

"That's the reason for the apprenticeship program. You will be taught how to sort the laundry under my strict, watchful eye," Helen said laughingly. "Now, what is on the schedule as far as our case is concerned?"

"I planned to give Peter a few hours to settle in at home, after his stint in the city jail, and then pay him a visit. We need to question him further about Leonard's social life,"

Hank replied. "Following that, we need to make a quick trip up to Little Rock to have a talk with Mr. Hegemon."

"Can't we just make a phone call to Hegemon to ask about the three thousand dollars?" Helen asked.

"I'd like to interview Mr. Hegemon in person to get a read on him. You can't very well tell if a person is telling the truth over the phone. You have to watch his reactions and mannerisms during questioning," Hank replied.

"OK, let me get the laundry together. We can get a bite to eat on the way to Ali's and after that head to Peter's."

Peter Driscoll lived in the same middle class area of south Shreveport as Ali and Preston. Peggy Driscoll answered the door to the modest two story colonial home. "Peter will be down in a minute. Please come in and have a seat," Peggy said.

"Mrs. Driscoll, this is my wife and investigative partner, Helen."

"It's a pleasure to meet you, Helen," Peggy said as they lightly shook hands.

A few minutes later, Peter Driscoll came down the stairs and greeted Hank with a robust handshake. "Hiring you was one of the best decisions I ever made, Hank. I know you'll find out what happened to my brother."

"My wife, Helen, here found the witness who gave us the information about the motorbike. I'm sure that was the bit of information that finally convinced Judge Mays to release you."

"Well, thanks to you, likewise, Mrs. Moran. Jail is one place I never want to experience again."

"Peter, it appears that the Shreveport P.D. might no longer pursue the case," Hank said. "Since your brother's murder took place in Claiborne Parish they might just let Sheriff Pettibone have jurisdiction."

"Oh," Peter replied. Hank and Helen waited for him to continue. "I'm afraid that my brother's case is going to fall through the cracks. I don't know how much experience Pettibone has in murder cases. I don't think there has been a murder over there since he was elected to office over ten years ago. Please promise me that you and Mrs. Moran will continue and find my brother's killer."

"We'll give it our best shot, Peter," Hank replied. "Now, there are some questions I need to ask about your brother's social life. And Mrs. Driscoll, I don't know how close you are with your sister-in-law, but some of these questions might be best answered by you."

"Sure, Hank, go ahead, we'll help in any way we can," Peter replied. Peggy nodded in agreement.

"Were either of you aware of Leonard and Susan's marital difficulties? I was told by Susan that she and Leonard had a scheduled meeting with a marriage counselor the Friday after Leonard's disappearance."

"I knew nothing about his marital difficulties until Peggy told me last month," Peter answered.

"I called Susan to offer my condolences after you found Leonard's body," Peggy added. "She did mention that she and Leonard had been having difficulties and that they had scheduled a meeting with a counselor. She wouldn't say what the actual difficulties were though."

"Both Leonard and Susan were having extra-marital affairs. Susan was seeing the plumber who lived across the street and Leonard was having an affair with a commercial artist named Lucy Chatham who did advertising work for the store," Hank informed the couple.

"Leonard was having an affair with Lucy Chatham? Unbelievable!" Peter exclaimed.

"Do you know how Leonard and Ms. Chatham met?" Helen asked.

"Leonard met her through a mutual friend at a business seminar up in Little Rock," Peter answered.

"Needless to say both Ms. Chatham and Mike Billings, the plumber, are on our list of suspects," Hank said. "Peter, do you know if Leonard had a large life insurance policy other than the one owned by the store?"

"Yes, we both took out large policies on ourselves at the same time we bought the store's policies. They were for five hundred thousand each. The reason for the large amount is because in our wills, the surviving brother gains full ownership of the store. The five hundred thousand would more than compensate the surviving family for not having any further interest in it." Peter answered. "You don't think Susan killed Leonard for the money?"

"Please understand I am only grabbing at straws and putting forth scenarios now," Hank explained. "If Susan was involved she might have had help from her plumber friend. He admitted he owns a motorbike. Detective Meyers promised to email some photographs of tire treads he found near the back of Leonard's truck. When I receive them I plan to compare the treads on Billings' bike to see if they match."

"So that's why detective Meyers asked if I owned a motorbike! He sure looked disappointed when I told him no," Peter said.

"Peter wanted to get one, but I wouldn't let him," Peggy added. "I told him in no uncertain terms that I would not take care of a paraplegic husband if he wrecked it and himself."

"I'm with you one hundred percent on that!" Helen said. "I gave Hank the same ultimatum when he wanted to buy a Harley."

"What are we going to do with these women?" Peter said laughingly to Hank. "They want to spoil all our fun!"

"Well, I think that sometimes they have a bit more common sense than us men. Soon after I wanted to get that Harley a good friend of ours laid one down on a slippery turn and shattered his right leg and arm. He never did fully recover. Still walks with a cane."

"Ouch!" Peter replied.

"One more question before we go," Hank said. "Peter, do you know the nature of a three thousand dollar payment that was made to the store from Hegemon Furniture Manufacturing up in Little Rock?"

"I saw that entry while checking the books after Leonard was killed. I thought the payment was odd because we usually paid Hegemon. I didn't have time to follow up on it though. Do you think it might be significant?" Peter asked.

"It could be," Hank answered. "Sometimes the seemingly insignificant things turn out to be important leads. We are going to head up to Little Rock tomorrow to have a talk with Mr. Hegemon."

"If you want me to, I can call Earl Hegemon tomorrow and ask about it," Peter volunteered.

"No, don't do that. I want to talk with Hegemon personally," Hank replied. "OK, we won't take any more of your time, Peter. We'll be sure to keep you informed of our progress."

"Thanks again for your help, Hank. I am sure you'll get to the bottom of all this."

"Hank, let's take the Bounder up to Little Rock. I would like to stay an extra day and see the Clinton Presidential Library," Helen suggested as they drove back to the campground.

"Good idea!" Hank said unexpectedly. "I don't see why we can't mix a little sightseeing along with our investigation. You know that I was never a big fan of the Clintons like you are, but I would like to see the library for historical reasons."

"Wonderful, I didn't think you would agree! I'll get online and make the reservations," Helen happily replied. "What about our reservation here at Tall Pines?"

"Well, we'll need to come back here after Little Rock," Hank answered. "I'll stop at the campground office on our way back to the Bounder to make additional reservations."

"Then we need to head to Ali's," Helen added. "She wants to have us over for supper. She asked if we had another shoofly pie and I had to tell her that you ate them all."

"Hey, it wasn't just me. If I remember correctly you had a few pieces yourself," Hank replied.

The following morning as they were passing through Hope, Arkansas on I-30, Hank's cell phone chimed indicating he had received an email. He handed the phone to Helen and asked her to check it out.

"It's an email from Detective Meyers. There's an attachment with a photograph of the trail bike tread marks. I see he laid a six inch scale beside the tracks to give a size reference."

"Good, I'll have to call Craig and thank him when we stop at the rest area above Arkadelphia," Hank replied.

"I always get uneasy pulling into rest areas since the murder of poor Mr. Soto at the rest area up in Indiana," Helen said.

"That was the start of quite an unexpected adventure," Hank replied.

"Won't we ever see the end of racial hatred?" Helen asked.

"I am afraid we won't see it in our lifetime," Hank replied.

When they stopped at the rest area, Hank punched the speed dial for Detective Meyers, who answered on the third ring. "Shreveport Police Department, Detective Meyers speaking."

"Craig, Hank Moran, thanks for the email with the tread pic."

"No problem, Hank. Glad to help."

"Craig, if you are still pursuing the case, you might want to check out the tire treads on Mike Billings' trail bike. He's the plumber who lives across the street from the Driscoll house. He and Susan Driscoll were having an affair. He wasn't too cooperative when I tried to talk to him. I doubt he would let me see the bike."

"Whoa, you're way ahead of me, Hank. You say that he and Susan Driscoll were an item?"

"That's right. Both Leonard and Susan were having extramarital affairs. They were scheduled to see a marriage counselor the Friday after his disappearance."

"You think maybe this Billings guy didn't want to lose Susan and eliminated Leonard from the playing field?"

"It's a possibility, Craig."

"OK, I'll check him out. I might have to get a court order from Judge Mays to see the bike though."

"Take a chance, Craig. He might be more cooperative when confronted by the police. If not, you can always go back with the search warrant."

"OK, Hank, I'll get back with you after I pay Mr. Billings a visit."

The Downtown Riverside RV Park was directly across the Arkansas River from the Clinton Presidential Library.

The RV Park was small but neatly maintained with all the expected amenities, including Wi-Fi. The site they were assigned was a back-in along the steep bank of the river.

"Look, you can see the Clinton Library across the river," Helen said as they admired the scenic area.

"Looks like an interesting building," Hank said. "I see they were smart enough to elevate the main floor in case of river flooding."

Hank had called ahead from the rest area and made an appointment to interview Mr. Earl Hegemon at three that afternoon. After having lunch in the Bounder, Hank and Helen set out in the Honda to find Hegemon's furniture business.

Hegemon's Furniture Manufacturing covered about a half city block on Asher Avenue on the southwest side of Little Rock. Hank parked in a spot reserved for customers and he and Helen entered through the double glass doors into the reception area and walked up to the counter.

"May I help you?" asked the petite blonde, blue-eyed receptionist.

"We have a three o'clock appointment to see Mr. Hegemon," Hank replied.

"Your names, please?"

"Mr. and Mrs. Hank Moran."

"OK, please sign in on the register and have a seat. I'll ring Mr. Hegemon."

Hank and Helen did as the receptionist requested. Five minutes later they were greeted by a short, stocky, balding man in his late forties. "Good afternoon, Mr. and Mrs. Moran, Earl Hegemon. I don't believe I have ever had the pleasure to talk with anyone in your profession."

"In that case we'll try to make it a memorable occasion," Helen replied with a smile.

"You stated on the phone that you would like some information on my company's dealings with Driscoll Furniture?" Hegemon inquired.

"That's correct," Hank answered. "We won't take up much of your time."

"Well, please, follow me. We can talk in my office." Hegemon beckoned.

Hegemon's small but efficient office was on the second floor of the facility and looked out over the production area. His desk was neatly arranged with a minimum of visible paperwork.

"Please, have a seat," Hegemon said as he motioned to the two chairs in front of his desk. "It's a real pity, what happened to Leonard," he continued as he took his seat.

"How long have you known Leonard Driscoll?" Hank inquired as Helen produced a pad and pen to take notes.

"I've known Leonard going on fifteen years. Our relationship started on a business level and over time we had become good friends. We are, or were, both fishing enthusiasts and we took turns fishing together either in Louisiana or up here in Arkansas," Hegemon replied.

"How often did you get together?" Hank asked.

"We tried to get together at least twice a year. Now I know you good folks didn't come all the way up here to talk about Leonard's and my fishing adventures. So what is your purpose in coming here?" Hegemon asked.

"We have been hired by Peter Driscoll to look into his brother's murder. The police dropped the charges against Peter and it appears their investigation is going nowhere. Peter wants us to fully clear his name by finding the person responsible for Leonard's death," Hank replied.

"I see, now what has all this got to do with me?" Hegemon inquired, a bit on edge.

"We are exploring every avenue we can find at this point in our investigation. Sometimes seemingly unimportant things can lead to a major breakthrough. So I'll get right to the point," Hank replied.

"Please do!" was Hegemon's response.

"Six months ago, there was a deposit into Driscoll Furniture's account in the amount of three thousand dollars. The money was from a check written by Hegemon Furniture Manufacturing. Normally Driscoll paid your company, Mr. Hegemon, not the other way around. What was the nature of that payment?" Hank inquired.

Earl Hegemon broke out in a wide grin and said, "Six months ago I was talking with Leonard trying to arrange a bass fishing outing when he said he would have to opt out because he was having difficulties in meeting his store's payroll. I offered to loan him some money, and after initially refusing my offer he decided to agree to it. He was a very proud man and it must have pained him to accept the loan. The loan was in the amount of three thousand dollars."

"That explains the ledger entry," Hank said. "However there was no following entry of re-payment."

"The Tuesday before Leonard's disappearance I received a Fed-Ex package containing thirty five hundred dollars in cash. Leonard's hand written note explained that the extra five hundred was for interest on the loan," Hegemon said as he reached into his desk drawer and pulled out a white envelope. "This envelope contains five hundred in cash that Leonard said was for interest and which I cannot keep. I have been meaning to return it to Peter Driscoll but I haven't had the chance or time. Would you please see that he gets it?" Hegemon requested.

"I certainly will," Hank replied. "And if you are interested as to why he sent you the money in cash, I believe I can explain that."

"Please do! I have wondered about that ever since I received it," Hegemon replied.

Hank explained, "Leonard had a bit of luck at a casino and won ten grand on a dollar slot. He made a deposit of sixty five hundred into the store's account. We have wondered what happened to the other thirty-five hundred, and now that little mystery seems to be solved."

"Wonderful, glad to be of help to you," Hegemon said.

"You've been a great help, Mr. Hegemon. Thank you for your valuable time and we'll make sure Peter receives the envelope," Hank said.

While walking back to the Honda Helen said, "I guess that shoots down the blackmail theory."

"It sure does," Hank replied. "It may seem like we are getting nowhere, but progress is made in a case with the elimination of each possibility."

"So, what is our next move?" Helen asked.

"Tomorrow we visit the Clinton Library, and then back to Louisiana," Hank replied. "Before we continue we'll have to check back with Craig Meyers to see if he had any luck with our plumber friend. If that lead doesn't pan out, we head over to Claiborne Parish."

"I have a feeling we'll be meeting Ms. Lucy Chatham," Helen said.

"Right you are Ms. Agatha," Hank answered with a grin.

Chapter 9

After a brief hop down I-30, Helen pulled the Honda into the parking lot of the Clinton Library at 1200 President Clinton Avenue. The library, located on twenty-nine acres with walking trails through the nicely maintained grounds, shared its grounds with the Clinton Foundation and the Clinton School of Public Service.

"After seeing the building from the campground I did some research on it on the Internet last night," Hank explained. "The library is a part of the National Archives. It has been designated as one of the most energy efficient and environmentally friendly buildings in the country. The U.S. Green Buildings Council awarded it a platinum rating under LEED, the Leadership in Energy and Environmental Design Green Building Program. It was the first federal building to receive a platinum rating, which is the highest LEED rating. Only twenty-nine other buildings in the world have achieved the LEED platinum designation."

"I always say the Clintons know how to do things right," Helen commented. "Why don't we splurge and opt for the hand-held audio self-guided tour of the library?"

After two hours of viewing exhibits they decided to grab a lunch of Low Country shrimp and grits with Red Eye gravy at the in-house restaurant aptly named Forty Two after the forty-second president of the United States.

Three hours later as they were leaving the building Hank said, "That was a very interesting tour, but they seemed to have forgotten something."

"What did they forget?" Helen asked.

"I didn't see one picture of Monica Lewinsky," Hank answered.

Helen sharply jabbed an elbow into Hank's ribs for this remark.

"Ouch! Did I ever tell you that sometimes you still take my breath away," Hank uttered as he winced in pain.

"When you recover I think we should stop and have dinner before we go back to the campground," Helen suggested.

"I'm OK now that you mentioned food!" Hank replied. "I heard about a place called the Capital Smokehouse and Grill. They're supposed to have the best baby back ribs in town."

"Sounds good! Let's go," Helen answered.

After returning from the restaurant, Hank's cell phone rang as they entered the Bounder. Hank saw on his phone's caller I.D. that it was Detective Craig Meyers on the line. "Good evening Craig, working late?"

"Hank, you know that we detectives love our jobs so much that we don't know when to quit," Meyers answered.

"Craig, you'll know when it's time to quit when you reach my age."

"I'm not that far behind you, Hank. By the way, I am accepting donations to my retirement fund."

"I'm afraid charity starts at home, good buddy," Hank replied with a chuckle.

"Hank, I paid a visit to your plumber friend Mike Billings this afternoon. I managed to catch him at his house in between plugged drain emergency calls."

"How did it go?" Hank questioned.

"Well, he was a bit belligerent at first when I told him I was investigating the murder of his neighbor, but he settled down when I told him it was just a routine visit. I told him he was on the list of possible suspects and that I needed to check his alibi for the time of the murder in order to remove him from the list. He seemed dumbfounded that he was on the list of suspects and demanded to know why. I told him it was because of his known affair with Leonard Driscoll's wife. At that point he uttered a few choice words on your behalf, Hank."

"Did he have a good alibi?"

"According to his records for Wednesday, October twentieth, he had a call for a stopped drain at five pm. Including travel time, the job took in excess of two hours. That was all verified by a call to the customer's residence."

"Hmm, the coroner's report stated that the time of death was difficult to determine considering the length of time that Driscoll's body was in the water," Hank commented.

"I know his alibi isn't rock solid but he would have had to have been an awful busy guy that day considering the drive time to the lake and all," Meyers said.

"I guess you're right. Did he let you see his trail bike?" Hank asked.

"Yes, after a slight protest he showed me into his garage. The bike was nearly buried in the usual accumulated garage paraphernalia. There was no match on the front or rear tire treads. Oh, and one other thing. He said when he came home from his Wednesday plumbing job he noticed Driscoll's boat was not in the empty lot or in his driveway. He admitted that he called Susan to see if they could get together but she said she was tired and that's when she told him about her and her husband's appointment with the marriage counselor. She then broke off her relationship with Billings. After talking to Billings, I went across the street to talk to Susan Driscoll and she verified Billings' phone call that Wednesday."

"Well, I guess that kind of wraps things up for possible suspects in the Shreveport area," Hank commented. "I always had the gut feeling that the solution lies over in Claiborne Parish."

"Have you been in contact with Sheriff Pettibone since the murder?" Meyers inquired.

"The last time I talked with the sheriff was when we pulled Driscoll's body out of the lake," Hank answered. "I am planning to head over that way as soon as we get back to Shreveport."

"Well, good luck in your investigation, Hank."

"Thanks, Craig, and thanks for the update. I'll be sure to keep you informed of any findings from my end."

When Hank ended the call, Helen asked, "Are we going back to Shreveport in the morning or do you want to head right over to Claiborne Parish?"

"I guess there's nothing else we can do in the Shreveport area. Why don't we head straight down to the State Park?" Hank replied.

"OK, I wanted to know because we are running low on groceries. If we are staying at the State Park we'll be eating in and we'll need to restock. Also, we'll have to cancel our reservation at Tall Pines in Shreveport."

"I'll call the campground first thing in the morning. Their office is closed now. Well, why don't we go do some grocery shopping and then stop for some ice cream," Hank suggested. "I'm still a little hungry."

"Why don't we stop for ice cream first and *then* do the groceries," Helen replied. "I know what you're like when you do the groceries while you're hungry. The Bounder's pantry and fridge will be overloaded."

"You're right again, sweetheart, though I didn't think I was *that* bad. Shall we go get dessert? I noticed a frozen yogurt store right near the Clinton Library."

"Mmm! Lead the way, Sherlock," Helen replied.

After the short trek back across the river, Hank and Helen enjoyed their cones of frozen yogurt and then headed to the grocery store near the highway interchange. Helen was amused that Hank restrained his habit of tossing extra items into the shopping cart and they left the Kroger grocery store with a manageable amount of supplies.

As Helen was putting the groceries away in the Bounder, Hank placed a call to Peter Driscoll. Peter answered on the third ring, "Driscoll Furniture, how can I help you?"

"Peter, this is Hank Moran."

"Hello, Hank, how's the investigation going?"

"We're still working on it, but I have some interesting news for you."

"Go ahead, Hank, what is it?"

"We paid a visit to Hegemon up in Little Rock yesterday and found out what happened to the rest of Leonard's casino winnings. Leonard sent the thirty-five hundred in cash to Hegemon for repayment of a three thousand dollar loan. Five hundred of it was for interest on the loan, which Hegemon said he could not accept since he and Leonard

were such good friends. He handed me an envelope with
the five hundred in it and said that I should see that you
get it."

"Well, I'll be. I tell you what, Hank, why don't you keep
the money as partial payment for your services. I know you
must be running up some expenses."

"I guess that I can live with that, Peter. If Preston is still
handling your books I'll give him a call so he can make a
record of the payment."

"Yes, Preston is still helping me out. Please call him for
me. So, is anything else going on with the case?"

"Well, so far we have eliminated all of the possible
suspects from the Shreveport area. We are about to head
over to Claiborne Parish to see Lucy Chatham."

"Do you think she was involved in Leonard's death?

"The two of them were an item and she is probably one
of the last people to have seen Leonard alive. He could have
broken the news to her that he and his wife were planning
to patch things up and she just might have gotten upset
enough to do him harm."

"It's hard to believe that Lucy could resort to murder.
She seemed like a very level headed individual in my
dealings with her," Peter replied.

"Peter, you know the old saying: 'Hell hath no fury like
a woman scorned.'"

"I know what you're saying, Hank, but I still can't
imagine that Lucy would do something like that."

"OK, Peter, we'll be heading over there for a few days to
nose around. We'll keep you posted."

After hanging up from Peter, Hank called his son-in-law
to inform him of the five hundred dollar payment.

"Hank, are you sure that the five hundred is enough?"
Preston asked.

"We're doing OK moneywise," Hank replied. "I'll make
up an invoice when we return from Claiborne Parish. We're
heading directly there from Little Rock to interview Lucy
Chatham."

"OK, Hank, I hope Ms. Chatham can throw some light
onto the investigation."

"I hope so, too, Preston."

After an early morning start the Morans left Little Rock behind and were nearing the Lake Claiborne State Park. "So, what's on the agenda for today?" Helen asked.

"First we better secure a campsite. The park might get busy with the weekend coming up," Hank replied. "Then, before we interview Lucy Chatham we better go see Sheriff Pettibone to let him know why we're in the area asking questions."

"Do you think the sheriff will be cooperative knowing we will be investigating a murder that happened in his jurisdiction?" Helen asked.

"I don't see why not. He seemed like an easygoing guy during Driscoll's body recovery in October. Besides, I don't think he was performing much of an investigation here at his end since the Shreveport P.D. zeroed in on Peter."

Ranger Murray recognized Hank when he walked into the ranger station to register for an RV campsite. "Mr. Moran, back to do some more fishing?" he asked.

"We plan to do a little fishing, but not the kind you might be referring to," Hank replied.

"I don't follow you," the ranger replied.

"We came over to Claiborne Parish to investigate the murder of Leonard Driscoll."

"I see, I thought the Shreveport police arrested his brother for the crime," Ranger Murray replied.

"Peter Driscoll has been cleared of any wrongdoing with regards to his brother's death," Hank answered. "In fact, we ran out of leads in the Shreveport area so we are shifting our focus closer to the scene of the crime."

"Why are you doing the investigating? I thought you were retired, Mr. Moran."

"I now have my P.I. license and Peter Driscoll has hired me to find his brother's killer."

"I see, and you think the murderer might be over here near Lake Claiborne?"

"I have always had that gut feeling," Hank replied as he noticed that Ranger Murray appeared just a bit uneasy when he answered his question.

"Well, if there is anything you need, please don't hesitate to ask," Murray replied.

"In fact, there is something I do need from you, Ranger Murray. I would like to sit down with you tomorrow at your convenience and go over your remembrance of the whole day before Leonard Driscoll's disappearance."

"That was over a month ago and things aren't as fresh in my mind as they were back then. Sheriff Pettibone questioned me thoroughly right after the discovery of the body. Perhaps you should talk to him," Murray suggested.

"I plan on seeing the sheriff this afternoon. I'll see what information he will part with related to his interview with you. I am sure I will have additional questions," Hank replied.

"Well, OK, Mr. Moran. Tomorrow at this same time would be good. Things won't pick up until the afternoon when folks start arriving for the weekend."

Hank noted the clock on the ranger station's wall. "That would be fine, Ranger Murray. Tomorrow at eleven a.m. is suitable. Now, we do need a campsite."

"Yes, I can put you in site twenty-seven. How long will you be staying?" Murray asked.

"Better make it for four nights. That will take us through the weekend," Hank answered.

"Four nights it is, Mr. Moran. That will be seventy-two dollars. Will that be cash or charge?"

Hank handed the ranger a hundred dollar bill that he had put into his wallet from the five hundred he received from Mr. Hegemon. *Easy come, easy go*, he thought to himself.

After receiving his change, a brochure with the campgrounds rules and regulations, and a short lecture on keeping the site clean from Ranger Murray, Hank returned to the Bounder to find site twenty-seven on the map.

"We have an appointment to interview Ranger Murray at eleven a.m. tomorrow," Hank said.

"I thought that Ranger Murray said he didn't see Leonard Driscoll at the boat launch ramp that day when Detective Meyers talked with him," Helen said.

"That's what he told Detective Meyers, but was he telling the truth? Unless it was his day off it's hard to believe he didn't notice Leonard arrive with his boat. He seems to keep an awfully close eye on visitors to make sure that they don't trash the place," Hank replied.

"It's too bad they don't have surveillance cameras," Helen said.

"That would make our job too easy," Hank jokingly replied.

"It seems like nothing is going easy with this case. We could use a little bit of a break," Helen said.

"Patience, my dear," Hank replied with a W.C. Fields intonation.

Chapter 10

Helen directed Hank to site twenty-seven with the aid of the map in the campground brochure. The site was one of the few pull-thru sites available in the park.

"This sure is convenient," Hank said as he motored into the site. "I noticed that the dump station is just down the lane. We might have to make use of it during our four day stay."

"If you don't spend your usual half hour in the shower we won't need the dump station until we leave," Helen chided.

"We are right next door to the shower house. I guess I could use the campgrounds facilities," Hank responded.

"All right! That way I'll get to enjoy some hot water in my shower. You always use it all up if you get in first," Helen said.

"Well, we better get this rig set up if we want to get into town to see the sheriff this afternoon," Hank said wanting to change the subject.

"OK, you get the outside hookups and I'll get the slides," Helen responded.

With the Honda unhooked and the Bounder set up, Hank entered the motorhome to clean some grease off his hands.

"We should have some lunch before we head into town," Helen said. "Would ham and cheese sandwiches be OK?"

"If you put a few of those jalapeno slices on mine," Hank answered. "While you make the sandwiches I'm gonna call Sheriff Pettibone."

After explaining who he was and his purpose for calling the switchboard operator, Hank was put through to the sheriff. The operator had informed the sheriff who was calling prior to connecting the line.

"Good afternoon, Mr. Moran. How are you and your grandson doing?"

"We're doing fine, Sheriff. Chip was OK once he got his favorite lure back."

"Well, finding a body like that could have been a bit traumatic for him, but I guess the priorities for a young boy are different than for you and me," Pettibone said with a chuckle.

"You're right, Sheriff. Since you mentioned priorities, would you have some free time this afternoon to talk about the Driscoll murder investigation?"

"I guess I could spare some time. Ain't much to talk about though. I'll be free in about an hour."

"Great, we'll see you in an hour. Thanks, Sheriff."

After having a quick lunch, Hank and Helen arrived at the sheriff's station on North Main Street in Homer just shy of an hour later. The twelve mile drive from the State Park took less than twenty-five minutes.

After a five minute wait while the sheriff finished a phone conversation, they were escorted into the sheriff's corner office. Hank noticed a picture on the office wall of Sheriff Pettibone shaking hands with former Governor Edwin Edwards, who had been sent to federal prison on federal racketeering charges.

"Good afternoon, Mr. Moran, and who is your lovely companion?"

"Sheriff Pettibone, this is my wife and investigative partner, Helen Moran."

"My pleasure," the sheriff responded as he lightly shook Helen's hand. "Investigative partner?"

"I guess we should explain," Hank said. "I recently opened a licensed P.I. agency and we have been hired by Peter Driscoll to find his brother's killer."

"I thought that case was all put to bed. Wasn't Peter Driscoll arrested for the crime?" Pettibone asked.

"He was, but Judge Mays set him free due to lack of sufficient evidence to hold him over for trial. His decision was mainly due to our investigation, which uncovered some information and witnesses that refuted the Shreveport P.D.'s evidence."

"I see, so the case is still open in Shreveport?"

"Well, Sheriff, I think the detective in charge in Shreveport has run out of suspects in the area and is relying mainly on your department over here in Claiborne Parish to handle it."

"So, Mr. Moran, I assume you are here to find out what we have found so far, and to tell you the truth it ain't much."

"Then can I assume that you have no suspects at the time?" Hank asked.

"Your assumption is correct, Mr. Moran."

"I was talking with Ranger Murray down at the lake this morning and he said that you interviewed him the day we found the body. Did he have anything of value to contribute?" Hank asked.

"Actually I talked with him the day after the incident. He said he had no idea how the body wound up in his lake. He further claims that he didn't even see Mr. Driscoll arrive in the park or launch his boat."

"I can't quite understand his claim that he didn't see Driscoll arrive. Activity must have been slow for a weekday in October and he usually keeps a watchful eye on things."

"Well he could have been in the crap—er ... taking care of nature. Sorry, ma'am," Pettibone said with a sheepish grin.

"No problem, Sheriff," Helen replied. "Actually it's OK to give recognition to one of history's great innovators."

Sheriff Pettibone looked at Helen with a confused expression.

"Thomas Crapper improved the functionality of the flush toilet that was invented by Sir John Harrington," Helen explained.

"I see, thank you for the history lesson, Mrs. Moran. I will be sure to pay homage to Mr. Crapper from now on," Pettibone laughingly replied. But Pettibone's mood changed abruptly with Hank's next query.

"Sheriff, Leonard Driscoll had been having an affair with a Ms. Lucy Chatham from over here in Homer. Along with talking with you, she is the other reason for our trip over here."

The sheriff's face suddenly reddened and he said, "Lucy had nothing at all to do with Driscoll's murder!"

"It sounds like you know Ms. Chatham," Hank replied.

"I should know her—she's my daughter. And like I said, she had nothing to do with Driscoll's murder!" Pettibone heatedly replied.

Hank was rendered momentarily speechless by the sudden revelation of the sheriff's relationship with Lucy Chatham. When he re-gathered his thoughts he continued, "Sheriff Pettibone, I am not accusing your daughter of being implicated in the murder. We need to talk with her because she might be one of the last persons to have seen Leonard Driscoll alive. Leonard might have confided in her about who might have wanted to do him harm."

Pettibone responded, "I have talked with Lucy and she has no idea who hated Driscoll enough to kill him."

"Sheriff, we're both experienced police officers and we both know that questioning by a family member may not be as objective as being questioned by an unrelated officer. I promise you that we will be discreet and highly professional in the matter."

Sheriff Pettibone considered Hank's offer before responding. "Mr. Moran, I checked into your background back in October and found you to be the best of professionals. I trust that my daughter's name will not be dragged through the mud and that you will live up to your reputation. You may take this as only a statement of my feelings, or as a warning, whichever may apply in the future."

"Sheriff, I assure you that a warning is not necessary," Hank replied.

Hank and Helen discussed the session with the sheriff as they drove back to the campground.

"I wonder what the sheriff thought about his daughter dating an older married man. We should have asked him his feelings on it," Helen said.

"I didn't want to stir that pot any more than necessary," Hank said. "He might have thought we were insinuating that he was a suspect in the crime. I thought it best to let him simmer down a bit."

"Well, depending on what he thought about his daughter's relationship with Driscoll he could be added to the list. It could be a fatherly rage sort of thing, doing what he thought best for his daughter."

"That's a possibility, pardner. Sheriff Pettibone should officially be on our list. I should have also asked him why he proudly displays a picture in his office of him shaking hands with former Governor Edwin Edwards, a known felon."

"Maybe Edwards is another relative of his," Helen replied.

"You have a devious mind, Mrs. Moran," Hank responded.

When they returned to the Bounder, Hank tried placing a call to Lucy Chatham, but after six rings her answering machine picked up, "You have reached the number of Chatham Creations. No one is here to take your call at this time. Your business is important to us so please leave a message and we will return your call promptly."

Hank replied, "Ms. Chatham, this is Hank Moran of Moran Investigations. It is very important that I get to meet with you at your very earliest convenience. You can reach me at this same number."

One hour later Hank's phone rang, "Hello, this is Hank Moran speaking."

"Mr. Moran, this is Lucy Chatham returning your call. My father said you would be calling."

"Ms. Chatham, it is very important that my associate and I meet with you to talk about your acquaintance with Leonard Driscoll. Are you free to meet this afternoon?"

There was a long silence then, "Yes. I really don't want to reopen the past, but it might be for the best. Why don't we meet at my place? How would three o-clock sound?"

"That would be 110 Edgewood Drive?" Hank asked.

"That is correct," Lucy replied.

"We'll see you at three then. Thank you, Ms. Chatham."

Hank drove by the sheriff's station on the way to Lucy Chatham's house. He noted that the sheriff's truck was parked in his reserved space. Hank was glad that Sheriff Pettibone would not be at Lucy's house to influence his daughter during the interview.

Hank and Helen pulled into the driveway of a small ranch house about a mile from the sheriff's station. The clock on the Honda's dash read three o'clock, the agreed upon meeting time. As they were exiting the Honda they noticed a Sheriff's Department patrol car slow down and stop directly across the street. The deputy who was driving had a cell phone to his ear and was looking toward the house.

Hank said, "It looks like the sheriff is keeping tabs on us or his daughter."

"He's not being shy about it either," Helen replied.

Helen rang the doorbell and the door was immediately opened by a brown haired woman talking into a cell phone that was pressed to her ear.

"It's all right, Richard. I'll be fine," she said as she ended the call and greeted her visitors. "Hello, are you Detective Moran?"

"Yes, I am, and this is my wife and associate, Helen Moran."

"I am Lucy Chatham. Won't you please come in?"

They entered the front room of the house, which looked more like an office than a living room. In the middle of the room was a large desk that held two computers wired to thirty-inch flat screen monitors and small inkjet printers. Along the back wall stood a large floor model printer.

Lucy beckoned the Morans to have a seat on a sofa across from the desk that was turned at a right angle to the wall while she sat on the chair facing it with a coffee table between them.

"My father said you want to ask about my relationship with Leonard Driscoll."

"Yes, we do," Hank replied. "We have been hired by Leonard's brother, Peter, to find the person responsible for his death. We apologize that we have to delve into your personal relationship with Leonard, but it might prove critical in solving the case. We also want you to know that any information we receive from you will be held in the strictest of confidence."

"You may ask any questions you wish," Lucy replied. "It is no great secret that Leonard and I had an affair."

"How did the two of you meet?" Hank asked.

"We were introduced to each other by a mutual friend at a furniture business seminar up in Little Rock about six months ago. I attended the seminar with the hope of making new contacts for my commercial artist business."

"If I may ask, what is the name of the mutual friend?" Hank inquired.

Lucy explained, "We were introduced by Earl Hegemon of Hegemon's Furniture Manufacturing. I designed some brochures and a letterhead for Mr. Hegemon. He was very pleased with my work and suggested that I attend the seminar where he could introduce me to potential new clients."

"How did you get into the commercial art business?" Helen asked.

"I studied commercial art at LSU, where I met my late husband. We were married right out of college. He wanted a stay-at-home wife so I never put my education to use until two years ago. Michael was in ROTC at LSU and two years after we were married his unit was called up for active duty in the Iraq war. A week before he was due to come home he was killed by a roadside bomb."

"That's so tragic!" Helen replied. "We are so sorry for your loss."

"After Michael's death it took a while to decide what to do with my life. My father suggested that I start my own commercial art business. He helped me invest in the equipment two years ago and here I am. It was slow going at first but business has improved lately."

Helen glanced at Hank who nodded for Helen to continue her line of questioning. He surmised that Lucy looked more at ease answering questions put forth by Helen rather than by him. "Did Driscoll Furniture aid in improving your business?" Helen continued.

"Yes, they did in a small way," Lucy replied. "Leonard called a week after we met at the seminar and wanted to know if I would be interested in creating a full page ad for a forthcoming furniture sale. I told him I was and that I could meet with him the next day. When we met the next day we seemed to hit it off right away. It was kind of weird in that I had the feeling that something was going to happen between us, and two weeks later we were dating."

"Did you know at that time that Leonard was married?" Helen asked.

"After our first meeting to discuss the spread for the newspaper ad I did some basic research and found that he was married. But for some odd reason it didn't matter to me. I just enjoyed being in his company."

Helen decided to get right to the point and asked, "Did you meet with Leonard the Wednesday that he disappeared?"

"Yes, I met with him that day at the lake. I actually didn't know that he had disappeared until my father called on the Saturday afterward and told me that his body was found in the lake. We had had no plans to meet that weekend."

"What time was it when you met him at the lake?"

"It was early afternoon, probably around two."

"What did you and Leonard talk about that day?"

"I saw the For Sale sign on his boat and asked him about it. He said that he wanted to sell it because he was tired of it and fishing didn't give him much pleasure anymore. He said someone was coming to see the boat. Then he told me the reason that he wanted to meet with me."

"And what was that?" Helen asked.

"He basically informed me that he planned to start divorce proceedings from Susan."

"How did you feel when he broke that news to you?" Helen inquired further.

"I was happy of course because I had fallen in love with the guy. My friends told me that I was wasting my time dating a married man and I should end the relationship. I was glad I didn't listen to them."

Helen continued the questioning, "I can imagine how you felt receiving news like that, Lucy. What happened next?"

"Nothing really, I cried a happy cry and told Leonard that I would be waiting for him and went to my car. As I was driving out of the lot I saw him backing his boat and trailer onto the launching ramp. That was the last I saw him."

At that point Helen noticed the mist in Lucy's eyes. "Lucy, did you notice anyone else near Leonard when he got into his boat?"

"Yes, I saw a man in a park ranger's uniform approach the ramp and stand to watch Leonard back the boat into the water."

Helen immediately turned her head and questioningly looked at Hank.

Hank asked, "Lucy, what did the man in the ranger uniform look like?"

"He was a tall man, taller than Leonard, with light brown hair," Lucy answered.

"Did you happen to notice the name on the ranger's nametag?" Hank continued.

Lucy responded, "No, I didn't. I was too far away to read it if I would have seen it."

"What happened after you saw the park ranger approach Leonard?"

"Like I said before, I was driving out of the lot when I saw the ranger. I just kept going and didn't see any more."

Hank then asked, "Did Leonard happen to mention who the prospective buyer was that was coming to see the boat?"

"No, he didn't say who it was."

Helen then took a chance to delve further into Lucy's personal life, "Lucy, what did your father think of your relationship with Leonard?

"He was upset when he found out about it," Lucy replied. "He didn't think it was proper for a young woman my age to date an older man, especially a married man. I think he was mainly upset because that young woman happened to be his daughter. He seemed to settle down when I reminded him that he was fifteen years older than my stepmom."

"How did he reply to that reprisal?" Helen asked with a smile.

"He just turned red in the face and said, 'Well, I guess you are your father's daughter.' Then he gave me a hug and told me he just wanted me to be happy."

"How long ago did your father find out about Leonard?" Helen continued.

"I think it was about two months ago," Lucy replied.

"Was your father OK with the relationship after that?"

"He seemed to be. Nothing more was said about it up until the time of Leonard's death. When he came and told me that Leonard's body had been found in the lake he seemed genuinely concerned for my feelings."

"Did he know at that time that the relationship between you and Leonard had turned more serious?" Helen asked.

"I don't think he did. He seemed really surprised when I told him about Leonard starting divorce procedures. He just said, 'Huh, how about that.'"

Hank could see out the front window behind Lucy that a sheriff's deputy patrol car had driven slowly past the house two times as they were interviewing Lucy. "It looks like your father is keeping tabs on you," Hank said. "I just noticed that the deputy who was out front of your house when we arrived drove slowly by your house again for the second time just now."

"Oh, that's just Deputy Mansfield," Lucy replied. "He has taken on the role of my personal guardian since my husband, Michael, died."

"The two of you must be good friends," Helen said.

"Well, I would consider Richard as just a friend. He asked me out on a few occasions but I always turned him down. I really don't want to go out with Richard. He's not my type, plus I think he would be somewhat domineering in a relationship. I told him that we should just remain friends."

"How did he feel about just being friends?" Helen asked.

"He said he really didn't have a problem with just being friends. He said he would still look out for me though."

"Lucy, did Leonard ever mention anyone who might want to do him harm?" Hank asked.

"No, he never talked about anything like that. He was always upbeat when we were together."

"OK, Lucy, thank you for talking with us," Hank said. "Here is one of my cards. If you happen to think of anything that would help us find the person responsible for Leonard's death, please don't hesitate to call."

"I surely will," Lucy replied.

As Hank and Helen were departing from Lucy's street they noticed Deputy Mansfield pass them from the opposite direction. "He sure is diligent in his promise to look after Lucy," Helen said.

"Does the term 'stalker' come to mind?" Hank asked.

"Yes, indeed it does," Helen replied. "It looks like we have another candidate for the suspect list."

"Yes, indeed it does," Hank replied. "By the way, I really liked how you were able to question Lucy about her father without letting on that he is a possible suspect. Lucy seemed very at ease in talking with you."

"Yes, it felt more like a mother-daughter chat. What about Sheriff Pettibone?" Helen asked. "I feel that he might be a little overprotective of his daughter, but I didn't get the feeling that he would resort to murder."

"It's hard to guess what a person's limit would be when confronted with a bad situation involving a loved family member," Hank replied. "Fortunately, Ali never gave us a reason to test *our* limits."

"So, do you think that in a heated argument type situation the sheriff could have struck Leonard and then tried to cover up his misdeed?"

"That is a possibility," Hank replied. "Plus we also have the fact that Ranger Murray lied about not seeing Leonard in the park that day. He could have been threatened and warned by the sheriff not to say anything."

"Then there is the possibility that Ranger Murray himself did the dastardly deed," Helen speculated.

"That is a possibility also," Hank replied. "But it would be hard to come up with a motive for him to murder Leonard. So far we haven't uncovered a tie-in between Ranger Murray and Leonard other than the fact that Leonard went fishing in Lake Claiborne."

Helen replied, "Maybe something will surface tomorrow when we question his lying about not seeing Leonard at the boat dock."

"It will be interesting to hear his answer," Hank replied. "After we get him to admit seeing Leonard launching his boat we'll have to ask if he saw anyone that was interested in buying it."

Helen then said, "Yes, one more suspect to add to the list, but this one is unknown. Our list sure grew in the short time since we arrived at the lake. Is this the way all murder investigations go?"

"Each one has its own momentum," Hank replied. "Some are easy and almost solve themselves, some you really have to work at, and ever so rarely there is one that never gets solved. This Driscoll case is one we have to work at, but I have a good feeling we are going to solve it."

"It does appear that the momentum is building," Helen said.

"Yes, it does," Hank replied. "When we get back to the Bounder I'm going to call Peter to ask if he knew about any interested buyers for Leonard's boat."

Then Helen had a revelation, "Hank, I just realized something! When we talked with Susan Driscoll she said that she and Leonard had an appointment at a counselor to try to save their marriage. Now Lucy just told us that Leonard was starting divorce procedures! Something doesn't add up."

"You're right, pardner! Somebody is lying. I have a gut feeling it isn't Lucy."

Helen replied, "So it was either Susan or Leonard."

"Leonard?" Hank questioned.

"Yes, maybe Leonard lied to Lucy about starting the divorce."

As Helen prepared a Polynesian chicken frozen dinner for two, Hank called Peter Driscoll on his direct line.

"Driscoll Furniture, Peter Driscoll speaking."

"Peter, Hank Moran. I have a question for you."

"Yes, what is it, Hank?"

"We know that Leonard was going to show his boat to a prospective buyer on the day of his disappearance. Did he happen to mention it to you and who it might have been?"

"No, I didn't know that he was going to show the boat to someone that day. I surely would have told the police if I did. I asked him if he was having any luck in selling the boat on the Monday evening that I changed his fuel filter and he said that he had had a few nibbles, but none serious."

110

"What about during the phone call he made to you at five o'clock to inform you about the furniture delivery?"

"No, he didn't mention anything then either. He only talked long enough to tell me about the delivery."

"OK, Peter. I was hoping you would have something. Sorry to bother you."

"No problem, Hank. Making any progress over near the lake?"

"We added a few names to the list of suspects including the mystery boat buyer. I expect to finish the investigation in a few days."

"Well, that's good news. Let me know if something breaks."

"You'll be the first to know, Peter. Oh, one more thing. Did Leonard mention anything to you about starting divorce procedures from Susan?"

"Divorce from Susan? No, Hank, he didn't. How did you come up with that?"

"Lucy Chatham said that on the Wednesday that Leonard disappeared he told her that he had started divorce proceedings. Is it possible for you to verify this with his lawyer?"

"I'll call him right away, Hank! I'll get back with you on it."

Chapter 11

After dinner, Hank was adjusting the batwing TV antenna to see what stations they could pick up. "I can only pull in two stations and one of them keeps going out. How about we watch a DVD?"

"There's really nothing of interest on TV on a Thursday night anyways," Helen said. "Let's watch *Grumpy Old Men*. It's always good for a few laughs and we haven't watched it since we got the Bounder."

Grumpy Old Men and its sequel, *Grumpier Old Men*, starring Walter Matthau and Jack Lemmon were the cult movies of the Moran household. The lines by Burgess Meredith, Jack Lemmon's feisty ninety-four-year-old father produced laughs no matter how many times they watched the film.

After the movie Hank was lying in bed and suddenly remembered, "I just realized that the weapon used to hit Leonard Driscoll over the head with was never found. Craig Meyers mentioned that there is a fire trail that leads out to the end of the point along the cove where we found Leonard's body. We have a few hours to spare before our interview with Ranger Murray at eleven tomorrow morning so why don't we hike out there after breakfast?"

Helen replied, "Since Detective Meyers knew about the fire trail he might have already searched the area for the weapon."

"He would have had a hard time finding the weapon on Google Maps," Hank replied. "Meyers never visited the lake. He found the fire trail online."

"You're kidding me!" Helen replied.

The next morning, with the aid of the state park map Hank had received when he registered the day before, they found the beginning of the fire trail. Helen was driving and parked the Honda in the small turn-in at the head of the trail.

"OK, the cove should be about a half mile straight ahead," Hank said as they started the short hike.

Twenty minutes later, Helen looked to her right through the trees and said, "I see water over there—it must be the cove!"

Hank responded, "OK, the tree where we found the body should be about two hundred yards straight ahead."

Five minutes later, Hank spied a footpath leading from the fire trail towards the water. The narrow footpath was only wide enough for one person, and knowing how Helen hated spiders, Hank led the way to clear away any webs that might be strung across it. They arrived at the shore of the cove on the south side of the downed tree.

Hank explained, "We found Leonard's remains just on the other side of the tree. I can still see a piece of Chip's fishing line that I tied fast to the tree to mark the location of the body."

Helen said, "This area looks like it is heavily used by shore fishermen. There's old bait containers lying around and a few floats caught up in the tree limbs."

"Not to mention beer cans also," Hank replied. "If Ranger Murray would see this he would throw a fit."

"OK, just what are we looking for?" Helen asked.

"We're looking for anything that would be heavy enough to hit someone over the head with, open a good sized gash, and knock that someone out. In my experience, killers tend to quickly get rid of the weapon over fifty percent of the time. So there is a chance that we might find something."

Helen headed north along the bank and Hank went south. Other than more plastic trash and beer cans, nothing else was found that could have possibly been used as a weapon.

"Well, either the weapon was kept by the killer or it was heavy enough to sink to the bottom," Hank surmised disappointedly after they met back at the tree.

"It's ten o'clock, Hank. We better start back if we want to talk with Ranger Murray at eleven," Helen suggested.

"You're right. I don't think we'll find anything out here."

As they finished their hike back to the road Helen remarked, "It looks like there's a flyer stuck under the wiper blade."

"What would anyone be advertising way out here?" Hank replied.

Helen retrieved the flyer, unfolded it, and remarked, "Uh oh, I don't think it's an ad." She handed it to Hank.

Hank read, "You are not wanted here. Go back home."

The note was computer type written and laser printed.

"It looks like we started to stir up the beehive," Helen said. "Whoever left the note doesn't want us poking around."

Hank held the sheet of paper up to the bright sky and remarked, "No watermark. Just normal bond printer paper that's impossible to trace."

"It could be checked for fingerprints," Helen suggested.

"At this point I don't know if we can trust the Sheriff's Department for a print analysis," Hank replied. "We might have to wait and take it over to Detective Meyers in Shreveport."

Helen remarked, "Well, one thing we can do is compare the font to what is set on the computer that was used to write the note. Usually the font isn't changed."

"Good thinking, pardner!" Hank replied. "All we have to do is get certain individuals to print us a short note. We could start with Ranger Murray."

Hank and Helen had to wait as Ranger Murray checked in a weekend camper. After he was finished he told his Assistant Ranger, Sally Rheims, to take over the registration counter as they followed Ranger Murray to his private office. Once seated in the office, Hank began his questions.

"Ranger Murray, the day after we removed Leonard Driscoll's body from the lake you were interviewed by Sheriff Pettibone and you stated that you did not see Leonard Driscoll enter the park or launch his boat the previous Wednesday. Do you still want to stick to that statement?"

Murray replied, "Yes, of course. Why would I not stick to it?"

"Ranger Murray, I have a witness who claims she saw a light brown haired man in a ranger's uniform approach the dock where Leonard Driscoll was standing by his boat. This was on the Wednesday that he was last seen alive. How many male rangers with light brown hair work with you?"

A look of defeat crossed Murray's face as he softly said, "I am the only one."

"I assume by your answer that you are admitting that you saw Leonard Driscoll here at Lake Claiborne on Wednesday, October twentieth."

"Yes, I saw Mr. Driscoll that day," Murray replied.

"Why did you lie to Sheriff Pettibone?"

Ranger Murray, with downcast eyes, thought a moment then said, "I was so upset about the finding of a body in the lake that I just didn't want to get involved at all. It was just too easy to lie and have no involvement. I just wanted to be isolated from the situation."

"I see," Hank replied. "You're involved now, Ranger Murray. You are a sworn officer in the State of Louisiana and it was your duty to answer truthfully all questions asked by Sheriff Pettibone. I am not going to immediately report your actions to him. I will leave it up to you and your own volition. Now, did you and Mr. Driscoll have a conversation when you approached him at the boat dock?"

"Yes, we had a short conversation," Murray replied. "I gave him my usual spiel about not throwing trash in the lake. Then I noticed the For Sale sign and asked him how much he wanted for the boat. He said he'd be willing to sell the boat, motor, and trailer for nine thousand. He said someone was to meet him here shortly to look at it."

Hank made a mental note that Ranger Murray's statement about a prospective buyer coming to look at the boat corroborated Lucy Chatham's statement made yesterday. Hank then asked, "Did you see the person who came to look at the boat?"

"Yes, I was on the porch of the station when the person arrived," Murray replied.

Hank realized he was going to have to pry the information out of Murray. "Did you recognize the person, and if you did, who was it? And if you didn't recognize the person, give me the person's description."

Murray hesitated while he decided how to answer the question then said, "The guy's name who came to look at the boat is Jed Wilcox. When Jed arrived I saw them talk for a while then they both got into the boat and motored out into the lake."

"Do you recall what time it was when Mr. Wilcox arrived at the boat?" Hank asked.

Murray replied, "Not exactly. It probably was a little after three o'clock. Soon after they took the boat out onto the lake I remember leaving for my dinner break. I always go at three thirty and leave Sally in charge until six."

"Did you see Mr. Driscoll and Mr. Wilcox return to the boat dock?" Hank asked.

"No, I didn't. Like I said I left for my dinner break. However when I returned to duty at six I noticed there were no boats or trailers in the parking lot. I assumed Mr. Driscoll had left."

Helen remained quiet up till now and then asked, "Ranger Murray, if you know where Mr. Jed Wilcox lives, would you please type out his name and address for us so we have it for our records? And if you know his phone number, please include that."

"Sure, I know where he lives, but not his phone number," Ranger Murray replied. "It will only take a minute."

"OK, we appreciate that Ranger Murray," Hank said. "While you are typing the address, I have a few questions for your assistant."

"You can question her, Mr. Moran, but I am sure she can add nothing to the information I just gave to you," Murray said.

Hank replied, "We have to try anyhow, Ranger Murray."

Hank and Helen left Ranger Murray's office and found Assistant Ranger Sally Rheims out on the porch of the station taking a smoke break.

Hank approached her and said, "Ranger Rheims, I am Detective Moran from the Moran P.I. Agency. My assistant, Mrs. Moran, and I have a few questions for you."

"Is this about Mr. Driscoll's murder?" Sally asked.

"Yes, it is," Hank replied. "On the Wednesday in October that Mr. Driscoll disappeared, Ranger Murray said he left you in charge of the station while he took his regular dinner break. When he returned at six he noticed no boats or trailers were in the parking lot. While you were in charge in his absence, did you see Mr. Driscoll return to the boat dock and leave the park?"

Sally replied not fully making eye contact with Hank, "No, I didn't. I was studying for my master's degree during that time and was fully engrossed in my studies. No one came into the station and I was unaware of anyone leaving the park."

Hank paused to think about what else he could ask when Helen chimed in after sensing Sally's discomfort. "How close are you to obtaining your masters?"

Sally smiled and said, "Please, call me Sally. I have one term to go for my masters in forestry management. I should have it by next spring."

"Do you plan to remain in Louisiana afterwards?" Helen asked.

Sally replied, "My dream is to land a position with the State of Colorado. Now don't tell Ranger Murray this because I believe he is expecting me to remain on here at Lake Claiborne."

"Your secret is safe with us, Sally. Now, we are in the black and gold Bounder up in site twenty-seven. If you happen to remember anything that could help us in our investigation, please stop in."

"I'll surely do that, Mrs. Moran," Sally replied.

Just then Ranger Murray came out onto the porch waiving a folded piece of paper in his hand, "Here's that name and address you wanted, Mrs. Moran."

"Oh, thank you, Ranger Murray, I do appreciate it," Helen replied.

"No problem at all, and if you need anything else just ask," Murray replied.

As Hank stepped off the porch of the station he happened to notice Ranger Murray's trail bike parked along the side wall and recalled how Chip had admired it in October. Hank had completely forgotten about it until now.

"Ranger Murray, do you mind if I check out your trail bike? My grandson admired it when he was here in October. He's getting to the age when he'll be begging for one."

"Sure, you're welcome to look at it, but it needs a new chain right now so you can't take it out for a ride," Murray replied.

Hank replied, "That's OK, I just want to get a feel for how heavy it is to see if he could handle one like it."

Hank sat on the bike, tilted it to one side and the other, and then lifted the front end up while gripping the handle bars. "Might be a little too heavy for him," Hank said. "I'm going to take a picture of it anyways for future reference."

Hank pulled out his cell phone and snapped a few pictures of the bike, making sure to include clear shots of the front and rear tire treads.

Hank waved his cell phone signaling thanks to Ranger Murray as he and Helen started the short walk back to the Bounder. Once inside, Helen quickly compared Ranger Murray's sheet containing Wilcox's address to the note that was left on their windshield. "No match," Helen said. "The fonts are different and also the paper looks like a different shade of white. The paper used by Ranger Murray looks darker, like it may be made of recycled paper."

"That makes sense with Murray being a gung ho environmentalist," Hank replied as he started to compare the shots he had taken of Murray's trail bike treads to the picture of the bike tracks emailed by Detective Meyers.

"Any match on the tire treads?" Helen asked.

"Looks like no match on the treads either. Murray's treads are knobby, strictly for trail, and the tracks sent by Craig Meyers look like treads that are used for street or trail."

"I guess that leaves Ranger Murray off the hook. Let's have lunch before we track down Jed Wilcox. I can make some ham and cheese sandwiches with some slices of that jalapeño pepper we bought."

"Mmm, sounds good to me," Hank replied. "I'd like to have a beer with it, too, but it feels like I'm still on the force and on duty."

"C'mon, Hank, I am sure there is nothing in the P.I. handbook that says you can't enjoy one beer for lunch."

"You know, you're right! A beer it is!

Chapter 12

Jed Wilcox lived less than five miles south of the park on Point Pleasant Road just west of Route 518. His double wide sat fifty yards back off the road and a well maintained gravel drive led up to it. It appeared to Helen that Mr. Wilcox took pride in his house and land as the grass was newly mown and the few shrubs were neatly trimmed. A black and white cat greeted the Morans on the front deck as they knocked on the door. The cat purred as Helen stroked its neck and back. "I hope Mr. Wilcox is as friendly as the cat," Helen remarked as the front door was opened by a short, thin, dark haired man in his late forties.

Before Hank had a chance to say hello, the man asked, "Are you the folks from Hammond Realty?"

"No, we aren't," Hank replied. "Are you Jed Wilcox?

"Might be, who are y'all?"

"We are private investigators from the Moran Agency. I am Hank Moran and this is my wife, Helen. We would like a few minutes of your time to ask you about your meeting with Mr. Leonard Driscoll up at Lake Claiborne this past October twentieth ... assuming you are Mr. Wilcox, that is."

The man thought a moment, stepped out onto the deck, and then said, "I'm Jed Wilcox. Is this the same Leonard fella that had the boat for sale?"

"Yes, it is," Hank replied. "Are you aware that Leonard Driscoll went missing that evening and his body was found in the lake three days later?"

"Huh, I heard somethin on the news about a body found in the lake. Ya sure he was the same guy that had the boat for sale?"

"Yes, he was, Mr. Wilcox. Tell me about your meeting with Mr. Driscoll."

"Ain't much to tell. We went for a short ride out into the lake, haggled about the price some, and then came back in."

"Was it a friendly discussion about the price?"

"I would say it was right friendly. He said he wanted nine grand and I offered him seven. Then he said that another guy was coming that same day to look at it and that he might consider my offer if the other guy wasn't interested. I assumed the other guy bought it cause I never got a call back."

"What time was it when you and Mr. Driscoll returned to the dock?

"I really can't say. We were to meet around three-thirty. We weren't out more than a half hour, so I'd guess it was around four or a little after."

"What happened then, Mr. Wilcox?"

"Nuthin happened. I gave him my phone number and left."

"Did you see anyone else arrive as you were leaving?"

"No, not down by the boat launch."

"Are you saying you saw someone else in the park?"

"Well, I passed a guy on a motorbike that was just turning onto the park road."

"Did you recognize that person?"

"He looked kinda familiar. A lot like Deputy Mansfield, but without the uniform so I really couldn't say it was him."

"Do you recall which direction he was coming from when he turned into the park road?"

"Now let me think." Wilcox made gestures with his hands in an effort to remember the direction. "Well I was goin out this way, and I am sure he was comin around from the right, so I'd say he was comin from the Homer direction."

"You said the rider looked a lot like Deputy Mansfield. How familiar are you with him?"

"I guess you could say a little too familiar. He wrote me up on a speeding ticket bout a month ago. I was only doin fifty-five in a forty-five zone. Cost me a hundred twenty bucks."

"OK, Mr. Wilcox, you have been a great help. I want you to have one of my cards just in case you recall something that would help in our investigation."

Hank handed Wilcox his card just as another car pulled into the driveway with a Hammond Real Estate logo on the door.

"Here's them realty fellas now," Driscoll said. "Gonna put the house up for sale."

"You have a nice place here, Mr. Driscoll. Why do you want to move?" Helen asked.

"I finally got me a weldin job over near Shreveport and it's too far to drive every day."

Helen replied, "Well, good luck on your new job. You should have no problem selling your house. It looks like you take good care of it. Have a nice day, Mr. Wilcox."

"Likewise, folks."

Hank nodded to the pair of realtors as he and Helen returned to the Honda. Once inside the car Helen said, "Well, I have the feeling that Wilcox was telling the truth."

"You're right," Hank said as he was backing out of the driveway. "I agree with you that Wilcox was being truthful. Besides, I couldn't think of a possible motive he would have for killing Driscoll. We know that it wasn't to steal the boat."

"It looks like Deputy Mansfield is right at the top of the suspect list if it actually was him that Wilcox passed turning onto the park road," Helen said.

"You're right again," Hank said. "Now all we have to do is prove he did it."

"I think we should have another talk with Ranger Rheims when we get back to the park," Helen said. "When you were questioning her before, I just got the feeling that she was holding something back."

"You may be right, pardner. I'm not about to doubt a woman's intuition. Especially the one sitting beside me," Hank replied with a smile and patted Helen on the leg.

"Keep that up, big boy, and we'll head right to the Bounder and forget about Ranger Rheims."

"Did I tell you how good you look in those jeans?" Hank replied.

"Flattery will get you everywhere, big boy."

Putting business before pleasure, Hank parked the Honda in the space beside the Bounder and he and Helen walked down to the ranger station to find Ranger Rheims. Rheims was busy checking in a camper when they walked in the door. Hank assumed that Ranger Murray was on his dinner break as he was nowhere in sight.

Helen noticed Ranger Rheims glance their way a few times as she was checking in the camper. Five minutes later the camper left with his site assignment and the brochure of the rules of the park.

Rheims turned to Hank and Helen and said, "Mr. and Mrs. Moran, how can I help you?"

Hank replied, "Ranger Rheims, we need to talk with you further about the day that Leonard Driscoll disappeared."

"I think I already told you everything I can remember," Rheims replied.

Noticing Ranger Rheims' unease, Helen said, "Sally, we only have a few additional questions. We won't take much of your time. And it is very important."

"OK, what do you want to ask?"

"While you were on duty that afternoon when Ranger Murray was on his dinner break, did you happen to hear or see anyone riding a motorized trail bike?" Helen asked.

"No, I don't recall hearing a trail bike on that specific day," Sally replied. "It is not uncommon to hear them though, so I could have."

Helen continued, "Did you see Deputy Sheriff Mansfield at all that day?"

Hank and Helen both noticed Sally's look of unease when questioned about Deputy Mansfield. Sally nervously replied, "I don't recall seeing Richard that day."

"Sally, you just called Deputy Mansfield 'Richard,'" Helen said. "It sounds like you are on a first name basis with him."

"Yes, he drops in a few times a week and we have become friends."

"Are his visits part of his routine patrol?"

"Yes, they are. If we aren't busy he stays to chat awhile with Phil and me."

"I see. Did he ever talk about Sheriff Pettibone's daughter, Lucy?"

"Oh, yes, he talked about her a lot. He has been trying to date her ever since her husband was killed. Phil used to tease him about it, telling him it wasn't a good idea since she was his boss' daughter."

"How did he take the teasing?"

"He got upset one time and told Phil that it was none of his business if he wanted to date Lucy. Richard had a real mean look in his face and Phil hasn't said anything about it since."

"Did Richard ever ask you out?"

"No, I think it was because he seemed to always have Lucy on his mind. I wouldn't have gone out with him anyways."

"Why not?" Helen asked.

"Well, he just came across as the domineering type. I really enjoy my independence and I just think that Richard would try to control me, or any woman for that matter."

"I see. Lucy Chatham had just about the same thing to say about him," Helen replied.

"Well, there you go," Sally said.

"Did Deputy Mansfield stop in at the station this morning?" Helen asked.

"Yes, he did. In fact, he asked if you and Mr. Moran were still in the park. I told him you were and gave him your site number," Sally replied.

"About what time did Deputy Mansfield stop by?"

"I think it was around nine-thirty," Sally replied.

"Did he say why he wanted to know if we were still in the park?"

"No, he didn't. I just assumed it had something to do with your investigation."

"Did you notice in which direction Deputy Mansfield headed when he left the station," Helen further inquired.

Sally answered, "He drove in the direction of the campground."

"Sally, like I mentioned earlier, if you remember anything that would help us in our investigation we are up in site twenty-seven in the gold and black Bounder."

124

"Yes, I know, Mrs. Moran. If I remember anything I'll let you know."

Hank had stood back and admired how Helen had a knack for putting people, especially other females, at ease. She wound up chatting with them and in the process extracted pertinent information. As they were walking back up to their site, Hank remarked, "Well, we now know that Deputy Mansfield is extremely infatuated with Lucy Chatham. Little pieces of the puzzle are starting to fall into place."

"We also know that Mansfield was in the park this morning about the time that someone left the note on our car," Helen added. "And we can also narrow down the timeline of the murder. If we believe that Jed Wilcox was telling the truth, Driscoll was alive at 4:15 when he dropped him off back at the dock."

"And don't forget Driscoll was still alive at 5:00 when he called Peter about the furniture delivery," Hank said.

"And when Ranger Murray came back on duty at six there were no boats or trailers in the parking lot," Helen added. "So that means he was murdered between five and six."

"We can narrow it down even further than that," Hank said. "It would take someone at least twenty minutes to motor back to the dock, re-trailer the boat, and leave the park. So we're talking about a time of death of between five and five-forty."

"That also means that the murderer had to park Driscoll's truck and trailer with the boat on it somewhere else before dropping it off at Driscoll's house at three a.m.," Helen said.

"Assuming we are focusing on the correct guy, we have to find out where Deputy Mansfield lives and check out his place. If he has no place to conceal the rig at his house maybe somebody saw it," Hank said.

"We sure could use another neighborhood snoop like Millie Hardwick," Helen joked.

As they were nearing the Bounder, they turned as they heard Sally call their names and run up to them. Speaking half out of breath she said, "I just remembered something else about that day!"

"What is it, Sally?" Helen asked.

Catching her breath, Sally replied, "After you asked me about hearing a motor bike I remembered hearing something else. I recall hearing a man and a woman arguing down near the boat dock and then the sound of a boat heading out into the lake."

"Do you remember what time that was, Sally?" Hank asked.

"I'm sure it was about a quarter to five. I remember looking up at the wall clock and thinking that I had over an hour to study before Phil came back from his dinner break."

Hank and Helen thanked Sally for the additional information and told her she had been a great help.

After Sally left they continued their walk up to the Bounder. Helen said, "I think it is safe to assume that it was Leonard who was arguing with the woman. No one else had a boat near the dock that afternoon."

"Assuming that Lucy was telling the truth about what time she left Leonard at the lake, it couldn't have been her arguing with him," Hank said.

"I am sure that our mystery woman won't turn out to be so mysterious in the end," Helen said.

"You have someone in mind?" Hank asked.

"Yes, I do, and it is most likely the same one that you have in mind," Helen answered.

Chapter 13

Four months prior

Deputy Sheriff Richard Mansfield was in his patrol car cruising North Main Street in Homer, Louisiana when he spotted Lucy Chatham's dark blue mustang pull into the parking lot of the Claiborne Chamber of Commerce. He tapped his siren button making two short blips, followed her into the lot, and parked his cruiser alongside her mustang. They exited their vehicles at the same time and Lucy asked coyly, "I'm sorry, Officer, did I do something wrong?"

"That depends on how you answer my questions, ma'am," Mansfield replied.

"And what is the nature of the interrogation this time, Officer?"

"The City of Shreveport has a very nice movie theater just waiting for the two of us to enter and enjoy the movie of your choice tomorrow night. Of course, this event would be preceded by a dinner at a fine restaurant. You are being requested to accompany this officer on the aforementioned evening."

Lucy was perplexed. Deputy Mansfield had asked her out on numerous occasions during the past year only to have to make up an excuse to turn down his request. This time she had a legitimate reason. "I'm sorry, Richard, I can't go out with you. I am seeing someone else tomorrow night."

Mansfield was momentarily stunned. He was sure Lucy's past rejections were based solely on the reason that she was still grieving the loss of her husband and was not yet ready to start dating. He had been patient and certain that she would eventually change her mind. Now she had just said she was seeing someone else. "Anyone I know?" Mansfield questioned in a less than happy manner.

"I don't think so," Lucy replied. "He is from Shreveport."

"What is his name? Maybe I do know him," Mansfield persisted.

"I really don't think you would know him. You'll have to excuse me now, Richard. I am already late for a business meeting," Lucy replied as she turned and walked into the Chamber of Commerce building.

Deputy Mansfield rapidly built himself into an angry state as he returned to his cruiser. He was seething and his cruiser squealed rubber as he exited the parking lot. The receptionist inside the Chamber had casually watched Lucy's conversation with the deputy through the plate glass front of the building. When Lucy approached her desk the receptionist asked, "What did you say to our gallant deputy sheriff, Lucy? He sure seemed to leave in a tizzy."

"Nothing earth shattering, Mary Sue. He just asked me out for a date tomorrow night, but I turned him down."

"I sure don't think he appreciated your answer."

"Oh, he'll get over it," Lucy replied.

The next evening, Mansfield parked his black F-150 pickup in the driveway of Homer Junior High School where he had a clear view of Lucy's house two hundred yards away on Edgewood Drive. He raised his digital SLR camera with the four hundred millimeter lens and aimed it towards Lucy's house. The lightly tinted windows in the truck afforded him some concealment but still allowed enough light to reach the long telephoto lens for a sharp picture of Lucy's mustang.

His wait was about twenty minutes when a gray late model GMC pickup truck turned into Lucy's driveway and parked behind her mustang. He snapped a picture of the back of the truck making sure the auto focus clearly showed the license plate number on the camera's LCD preview screen.

The camera clicked in rapid succession as the driver exited the truck and walked to Lucy's front door. When the door opened, Mansfield witnessed Lucy embrace the man and with anger rapidly building he continued to snap pictures as the couple walked to the man's truck. The man opened the truck door for Lucy and held her hand as she stepped up into the cab.

Mansfield followed the GMC as it turned west onto Main Street and then south on 79 towards Minden. Not wanting to risk detection, he gave up the tail and headed back to his double wide trailer on Hill Street. Once at home, he downloaded the series of photos onto his laptop and brought up the one showing the truck's license plate. He cropped the picture to show only the rear of the truck and printed the resulting image on plain bond paper. With the photo of the license plate in hand, he headed to the sheriff's station on North Main Street.

As he entered the station, Evelyn Hawkins, the night dispatcher, spoke. "Richard, what are you doing here so late? Wasn't your shift over at four?"

"Yes it was, Evy, but I remembered there was a plate I had to run this afternoon. It just slipped my mind."

Mansfield sat down at a desk and brought up the DMV database on the station's dedicated terminal. He entered the tag number from the pickup truck that was in the picture and waited for the results. Ten seconds later the data appeared. The tag number corresponded to a gray, 2010, GMC pickup, owned by a Mr. Leonard Driscoll who lived on Ridgewood Drive in Shreveport. He then accessed Leonard Driscoll's driver's license information, which gave the same address as the truck registration and listed his age as forty-two years old.

Lucy, why are you dating someone over ten years older than you? he thought in anger as he logged off of the terminal.

Back at home, he booted up his laptop and googled Leonard Driscoll, Shreveport, Louisiana. The fourth listing was for Driscoll Furniture with Leonard Driscoll and Peter Driscoll listed as owners. He clicked on the link and the Driscoll Furniture Web site downloaded. On the site's homepage was a photograph of Leonard and Peter Driscoll standing at the entrance to the Driscoll Furniture store. He then clicked on the history tab and learned that the store was opened in 1979 by William Driscoll, and upon his death in 1999, was managed by his two sons, Leonard and Peter.

Mansfield then searched for the telephone listing for Leonard Driscoll in the online white pages directory. The listing that appeared was for Leonard and Susan Driscoll. *The asshole is married*, he thought as he dialed the number. A woman answered the phone, "Driscoll residence."

"Hello, is this Mrs. Driscoll?" Mansfield asked.

"Yes, it is. Who is calling?"

"I am a friend of Leonard's. May I speak with him, please?

"I'm sorry, Leonard isn't home."

"Do you expect him back soon?"

"No, he usually gets in late. It's his poker night."

"Oh, that's right. I forgot about that. Is the game at the usual place?"

"I am not sure. He usually plays at Diamond Jack's."

"That's right! Maybe I'll just head on up there myself. Have a good evening, Mrs. Driscoll."

Mansfield ended the call then mumbled to himself, "Poker night my ass!"

Leonard wasn't lying to his wife when he said he was going out to play poker. He just neglected to mention that he would be accompanied by a young and pretty female named Lucy Chatham. Leonard treated Lucy to a steak dinner at Diamond Jack's Casino and after dinner was surprised when Lucy said she would accompany him to the poker table. In fact, she said that she would also like to play as she had learned the game from watching her father during many of his Friday night poker games.

Leonard never played at the high stakes table. He just enjoyed playing the game in the atmosphere of the casino as he relished it more than a friendly game at one of his buddy's houses.

Leonard lost a grand total of fifty dollars that night, however, to his surprise, Lucy won eighty. It seemed to him that he had found the perfect partner in life; someone who also enjoyed the game.

Two weeks later, Leonard and Lucy made arrangements to once again enjoy an evening out at the casino. Lucy told

Leonard that she would meet him at the casino as she wanted to save Leonard the numerous trips to Homer and back. After a mild protest, Leonard agreed to the arrangement.

They embraced as they met in the parking lot unaware they were being photographed in the brief intimate act. Mansfield exited his truck once the couple had entered the casino. He had to leave his SLR camera with the big lens inside his truck as cameras were not permitted inside the establishment. He reckoned he could fake talking on his cell phone and snap the pictures he desired.

Mansfield spied the couple at the Texas Holdem table. Their backs were turned to him as they faced the dealer with the nametag "Bernie." Mansfield found a position far to the right of the table that afforded him a profile of Leonard and Lucy studying their dealt hands. He pulled out his cell phone and pretended to be talking to a caller, found the picture button, briefly held the phone away from his face to check the display screen, then snapped two photographs. With his mission accomplished, he strode out of the casino with a satisfied grin and drove back to Homer.

He had some time to think about his next move during the drive home. Should he confront Leonard directly with the photographs and threaten to show them to his wife if he didn't break off his affair with Lucy? Or should he arrange a meeting with Mrs. Driscoll and show her what her husband had been up to?

He opted for the second plan of action thinking it was exactly what the bastard deserved. However, that plan would have to be put on hold as a series of burglaries in the town and the surrounding parish demanded the department's full attention. All deputies were ordered to be available on a moment's notice, 24/7, to assist, if necessary, in the pursuit and apprehension of the burglary ring members. The orders also consisted of all-night stakeouts and increased patrols.

Chapter 14

Present day

"I think we should have another meeting with Sheriff Pettibone," Hank said as he and Helen entered the Bounder late in the afternoon.

"Do you think he knows about his deputy's interest in Lucy?" Helen asked.

"I don't know. We'll bring it up if the situation calls for it when we meet with him," Hank answered as he punched the speed dial for the sheriff on his cell phone.

The call was answered by the now familiar voice of the sheriff's secretary, "Claiborne Parish Sheriff's Office."

"Hello, Sheriff Pettibone, please. Would you please tell him Hank Moran is calling about an update on the Leonard Driscoll murder?"

"Sure, one moment please."

Ten seconds later, the sheriff came on the line. "Mr. Moran, my secretary says y'all have an update on the Driscoll case."

"Hello, Sheriff. Yes, we do. If you have a spare moment we would like to drop by your office for a brief meeting."

"Yes, you can if you make it here soon. I'll be leaving at five."

"We'll head right over. We should be there in fifteen minutes," Hank replied.

When the Morans entered the sheriff's station they were told by the sheriff's secretary, Ruth Morgan, that Sheriff Pettibone was expecting them and that they should go directly to his office.

Once again seated in front of the large man's desk they related their latest findings in regard to the Driscoll murder, including the interview with Jed Wilcox and the possible timeline of the crime.

"Sheriff, Jed Wilcox stated that he saw Deputy Mansfield, riding a trail bike, turn into the park as he was leaving on the day in question. Wilcox said he left the park at about four-fifteen. As we said before, we narrowed the possible time of the murder to between five o'clock and five-forty. This puts Deputy Mansfield in the area near the time of the murder. And another thing—a witness stated that she saw someone park Driscoll's boat in his neighborhood at three a.m., the night of the murder, and leave on what sounded like a trail bike."

"Mr. Moran, what possible motive could my deputy have for killing Leonard Driscoll?"

Hank replied, "Sheriff, are you aware that Deputy Mansfield is very interested in your daughter, Lucy, and asked her out on dates on numerous occasions, which she always turned down?"

"I was not aware of that. Did you get this information from Lucy?"

"Yes, we did. She didn't want to tell you for fear that you might get angry with Mansfield."

"She was right! I would have fired the bastard! Please excuse the language, ma'am."

"You're excused," Helen replied.

Hank continued, "Sheriff, we have a photograph of the bike treads left at the scene in front of Driscoll's house and we need to compare the tread design with Mansfield's."

"That should be easy," Pettibone replied. "His bike is parked out back. He occasionally rides it to the station instead of his pickup. Let's go check it! It should be easy to put this matter to rest."

Hank and Helen followed Sheriff Pettibone out the back door of the station to where Mansfield's bike was parked. Hank brought up the tread picture on his cell phone and held it beside the front tire on Mansfield's bike.

"Bingo, an exact match!" Hank said in excitement.

Hank showed the picture to Pettibone for a second opinion and the sheriff agreed on the match of the tread pattern.

"Sheriff, we know that Driscoll's boat and trailer were not at the park after six o'clock p.m. the day of the murder. This means that the rig had to be parked somewhere else

133

before it was delivered to Driscoll's neighborhood at three a.m. Is there a place where Mansfield could have hidden the boat for that period of time?" Hank inquired.

"Well, he lives in a trailer park, which is fairly open. However he could have parked it at his mother's place down near the park. The place is fairly secluded."

"Perhaps we should go and talk with his mother," Helen suggested.

"Not possible, ma'am," Pettibone replied. "His mother passed on about a month ago. Deputy Mansfield is in the process of moving into the house."

"Could you check to see if Mansfield was on duty on the day in question?" Hank asked. "That was Wednesday, October the twentieth."

"Sure can. Follow me," the sheriff said. "Ruth, would you please pull up the roster for October twenty and check to see if Mansfield was on duty that day?" Pettibone asked his secretary on their way back to his office.

Five minutes later, Ruth came into the office with the information. "Mansfield was off duty that day but was called in at six-fifteen to help cover the emergency of that crazy guy holed up in the courthouse who took the judge as hostage," Ruth related.

That's right! I remember that now!" Pettibone said. "The situation was cleared a little after midnight."

"That would give him about three hours to get back home and drive the boat rig to Shreveport by three a.m." Hank said. "That surely was enough time."

"I am afraid you're right," Pettibone said. "It appears we need to have a chat with my deputy."

"One other thing, Sheriff. We found a threatening note this morning on the windshield of our car after we returned from a hike out the fire trail to the site where the body was found. We think it was placed by Mansfield. The park ranger said that Mansfield was in the park at the time."

"Do you have the note with you?" Pettibone asked.

Helen retrieved from her purse the plastic bag containing the note and handed it to the sheriff.

"Ruth, would you please check the terminal that Mansfield usually uses and see if this note is still in the word processor," Pettibone ordered as he handed the note to his secretary.

A few minutes later, Ruth returned to Pettibone's office. "I couldn't find the note in the documents file, so I checked the deleted files and there it was. He apparently forgot to empty the computer's trash bin. I printed out another copy for you and saved the file."

"Good work, Ruth," Pettibone said. "Now, have Miss Hawkins radio Deputy Mansfield and have him report to the station immediately."

Chapter 15

Two and a half months prior

Mansfield had been saving the pictures he took of Leonard Driscoll and Lucy for nearly a month, waiting for some free time to present them to Susan Driscoll. Now that the burglary cases had been solved he had three days of comp time due to him. He had managed to occasionally check on Lucy's house and witnessed Leonard picking her up at the same time on two different Friday evenings. Being on call at a moment's notice from the Sheriff's Department, he wasn't able to risk the time to tail them back to Shreveport or to wherever they were headed for their rendezvous. However, he did manage to add a few additional snapshots to the collection.

Susan Driscoll answered on the third ring, "Driscoll residence, Susan speaking."

"Mrs. Driscoll, this is Deputy Sheriff Mansfield from over in Claiborne Parish. I was hoping you could spare some time for a short meeting today. I have something to show you that you would be highly interested in seeing."

"Is this some kind of crank call? What could you possibly have that I would be interested in?"

"Mrs. Driscoll, let me just say that your husband's Friday night poker games are a bit more interesting than he would lead you to believe."

"So, what did he do? Stop off at a strip club and have a lap dance or something?"

"Ma'am, I was going to wait to tell you until I showed you the photographs, but I'll come right out and tell you that your husband has been in the company of a young woman every Friday night for the past five weeks."

"You are really a deputy sheriff?"

"Yes, ma'am, you may call the Claiborne Parish Sheriff's Office and verify my employment there."

"I don't think that's necessary. How soon can we meet?"

"Well, ma'am if I leave home now I can be there in just over an hour. Where would you like to meet?"

"You can come to the house. Leonard will be at the store all day. Do you need directions?"

"No, ma'am, I have your address from your husband's driver's license information. I'll see you in an hour."

"Don't get a speeding ticket, deputy."

"I'll try not to, ma'am, however I do have connections."

The last picture was inching out of the photo printer as Mansfield ended the call to Susan Driscoll. He stuck the dozen pictures in an envelope and headed out the door. One hour and seven minutes later he pulled into the Driscolls' driveway, walked up to the front door, and knocked.

Susan Driscoll answered the door wearing tight fitting designer jeans and a tucked in white cotton blouse. She had recently obtained a new, shorter hairdo at Angie's Beauty Shop so her diamond pendant earrings accentuated her now bare neck. "Deputy Mansfield, I presume?"

"Yes, ma'am," Mansfield replied as he showed his badge. He was not in uniform and showed his badge to ensure his credibility. He was struck by Susan's beauty and immediately wondered why her husband would want to cheat on her.

"Come in, Deputy Mansfield, and have a seat. I am anxious to see what you have in that white envelope."

"Please call me Richard, ma'am," Deputy Mansfield said as he entered the home. "Before I show you the photographs I think I need to explain how I came about taking them."

"Richard, please call me Susan. Ma'am or Mrs. Driscoll sounds entirely too old."

"OK, Susan, the woman in the photographs is the daughter of my boss, Sheriff Pettibone. I have been trying to date her for the past eighteen months but was always turned down. I had thought it was because she was not yet ready to start dating after the death of her husband in Iraq. The last time I asked her out she told me she was seeing someone else. When I found out who it was and that he was ten years older than her and married, it just wigged me out."

"So, you followed them and took pictures for revenge?"

"No, not for revenge. I am still very interested in Lucy and only want the best for her."

"You said her name is Lucy?"

"Yes, I did. Her married name is Chatham."

"Lucy Chatham. I know who she is," Susan said. "She has been doing some digital ad work for my husband's furniture store. Well, Richard, let me see the pictures."

Mansfield handed the envelope to Susan and watched as she viewed the photographs, one by one, pausing at the ones that showed the couple embracing. After viewing the photos, Susan sat back in her chair and said, "Richard, you have no shots of them entering a motel or hotel room. Did you happen to see them doing anything other than playing poker together?"

"On the two latest occasions that he came to her house she invited him in instead of them leaving together in his truck. I drove by her place three hours later and his truck was still in her driveway. As far as I could see the only light that was on was in the front entryway."

"I see. He did come home quite late the last two Friday nights," Susan replied showing little emotion.

Mansfield stood and said, "I am sorry that you had to find out like this, but I thought you needed to know. I'd better be leaving now."

Susan arose and said, "Please don't run off so soon, Richard. Can you stay and have a drink?"

"I suppose I can. I have the day off and have no need to hurry back home."

"Wonderful! I'm in the need of a stiff martini. What would you like, Richard?"

"A cold beer would be just fine with me."

Mansfield could hear Susan mixing her martini in the kitchen. He heard the refrigerator door open and close and recognized the familiar sound of a longneck being uncapped.

"In here, Richard," Susan beckoned from the kitchen.

Susan turned to him as he entered the kitchen and he immediately noticed that the first few buttons of her blouse were undone revealing inviting cleavage.

She looked into his eyes, handed him his beer and said, "Please enjoy."

He sensed the possible double meaning of her statement and said, "Susan, you are a very beautiful woman. For the life of me I can't understand why your husband would be looking elsewhere."

"Richard, some men just don't realize when they have a good thing. In Leonard's case, I think it is just temporary infatuation."

"I believe I am becoming a little infatuated myself," Mansfield said.

"I was hoping that would be the case," Susan said as she set her drink on the counter, reached up and crossed her hands behind his neck, drew him close, and kissed him forcefully on the lips.

The kiss continued as Mansfield reached between their bodies, opened the remaining three buttons on Susan's blouse, and pulled it up and out of her jeans. She withdrew only long enough to let the blouse fall to the floor as she looked longingly into his eyes. He drew her close once again and made quick work of unhooking the three clasps on the back of her bra.

With a light pleasurable moan Susan softly said, "Richard, I think we would much more comfortable in the bedroom."

As she led him down the hall she thought to herself, *What's good for the gander is also good for the goose.*

Chapter 16

Present day

Deputy Richard Mansfield arrived at the sheriff's office fifteen minutes after the request to return to the station. He approached the night dispatcher Evelyn Hawkins and asked, "What's up, Evy?"

"Cecil wants to see you in his office immediately," she replied.

Mansfield walked by Ruth Morgan's desk and was about to speak when she motioned with her thumb to direct him to Pettibone's office.

He paused in front of his boss' door, knocked, and heard the sheriff's rough voice say, "Come in."

When he entered the office he noted the Morans sitting in front of the sheriff's desk and asked, "What's up, Cecil?"

"Pull up a chair and have a seat. You have a bit of explaining to do," Pettibone said.

As Mansfield obtained a chair from along the wall, Hank and Helen scooted their chairs to one side to make room for the deputy.

"Deputy Mansfield, I don't know if you have met these people," Pettibone said. "They are Mr. and Mrs. Hank Moran from the Moran Investigations Agency."

"I've seen them around the area but I haven't met them yet," Mansfield replied.

Hank arose from his chair and shook Mansfield's hand. Mansfield nodded to Helen, who was seated on the far side of Hank. When both men were re-seated, Pettibone continued, "Richard, these people have uncovered some very interesting details relative to the murder of Mr. Leonard Driscoll back in October. It appears that you may have an involvement in Mr. Driscoll's demise."

Mansfield replied, "I've never even met Leonard Driscoll! How could I possibly be involved?"

"A bike tread imprint that was left behind Driscoll's truck was photographed by the Shreveport P.D. and Driscoll's truck mysteriously showed up in front of his house at three the morning after he was murdered. A witness stated that she saw someone who might have been wearing a uniform unhitch the boat and trailer and move the truck to the front of Driscoll's house. She then heard the sound of a small bike engine leave the area. The bike tread matches exactly the tread on your bike that is parked out back. How do you explain that?"

Mansfield countered, "Cecil, the same make of tires is used on half of the trail bikes in the area. The fact that the treads match is no big deal."

"Richard, we have a witness who saw you enter the state park on your bike a short time before Driscoll was murdered. That puts you near the scene at just the right time."

"Cecil, that's just a coincidence," Mansfield replied. "I occasionally go riding in the park on my days off. I might have been in the park that day, but I had nothing to do with Driscoll's murder."

Pettibone picked up the copy of the note that was left on the Moran's windshield, placed it in front of Mansfield, and asked, "What explanation do you have for this?"

Mansfield replied, "I admit that I wrote the note and put it on their car."

"Why?" Pettibone asked.

"I just didn't like the idea of them snooping around where they have no business," Mansfield replied. "I didn't threaten them or anything. I just meant for them to go back home and to leave the police work to us."

"That act was very childish, Deputy," Pettibone replied. "The Morans have every right as licensed private investigators in the state to conduct their search for Driscoll's murderer. They have uncovered a lot of information that will lead to the solving of this case. They will continue to work very closely with this department and share any further information they might uncover with us. Do I make myself clear, Deputy Mansfield?"

"Yes, sir," Mansfield replied.

"May I ask Deputy Mansfield a question?" Hank asked.

"Go ahead, Mr. Moran," Pettibone replied.

Hank turned to the deputy and asked, "When you were in the park that afternoon just before Driscoll's murder, did you happen to hear a man and a woman arguing and then a boat leave the dock?"

Hank noticed a slight discomfort in Mansfield's demeanor before he answered the question.

"No, I didn't," Mansfield replied. "If I was actually riding in the park that day I would have headed directly to the trails and would have bypassed the dock area."

"You were called into duty the night of the hostage situation at the courthouse. I believe Sheriff Pettibone said the situation was resolved at midnight. Where did you go after you were no longer needed at the scene?"

Once again Hank noticed discomfort in Mansfield when he answered, "I went directly home and went to bed."

"Any further questions, Mr. Moran?" Pettibone asked.

"No, not at this time," Hank answered.

Pettibone turned to Mansfield and said, "Deputy Mansfield, I have half a mind to put you on administrative leave until this investigation is resolved, but I am going to let you continue on your job. One more thing ... stay away from my daughter!"

Mansfield was startled like he had been shot when he heard the sheriff's last order and meekly replied, "Yes, sir, I will."

After Mansfield left the office Pettibone asked, "Well, Mr. Moran, what do you think?"

"I think you were correct in letting him continue on his job," Hank said. "What we have uncovered so far is very circumstantial. However, I did detect a bit of discomfort when I asked him if he heard the man and woman arguing at the park and when I asked where he went after the situation at the courthouse. In my thirty some years of experience in questioning and reading people I can't say for sure if he was telling the complete truth."

"You think he might be hiding something?" Pettibone asked.

"There is that possibility," Hank replied. "I noticed you have pictures of all your personnel hanging up in the department. Do you mind if I take a snapshot of

142

Mansfield's picture with my cell phone? I would like to show it to someone."

"If you think it would help go right ahead," Pettibone answered.

"Thank you, Sheriff."

Hank snapped the picture of Mansfield's photograph as they were leaving the station. When they returned to their car Helen said, "I have a feeling I know where we're headed next."

"And where is that, pardner?" Hank asked.

"To see Millie Hardwick!" Helen answered.

"Bingo!" Hank replied. "We just have to keep chipping away. I feel certain we are getting close to solving this thing."

Just then Hank's cell phone rang and he saw on the display that it was Peter Driscoll calling. "Hello, Peter," Hank said.

"Hank, I just heard from Leonard's attorney. As it turns out, Leonard was starting divorce proceedings from Susan. He said Leonard came to see him the Monday before he went missing. He drew up some papers for him to sign and mailed them to Leonard's house the next day. The papers probably reached Leonard's house on that Wednesday."

"Peter, do you happen to know what time of day the mail is delivered to Leonard's neighborhood?" Hank asked.

"Gee, I did hear him say one time that he gets his mail at home early to mid-afternoon."

"Then it might have been possible that that Wednesday's mail arrived at his house after he left for the lake," Hank said.

"I see what you're getting at," Peter said. "You think Susan might have opened the mail from Leonard's attorney and found out about the divorce proceedings."

"That's a possibility," Hank said. "Thanks for the information, Peter."

"No problem, Hank. Glad to be of help. How is the investigation going?"

"I think we're getting real close to solving this, Peter. We'll let you know the minute we do."

Helen was able to get the gist of the one-sided conversation and when Hank ended the call she said, "It sounds like we are also going to pay a visit to Susan Driscoll."

"Not right away," Hank said. "Let's talk with Millie Hardwick first, then depending on what she has to say, we may want to get Detective Meyers involved."

"Should we leave the Bounder here or move it back to Shreveport?" Helen asked.

"I think we should leave it here for the time being," Hank said. "I have a feeling that we'll be headed back over here real soon. If need be, we can spend a night at Ali's. Let's get a bite to eat and head back to the park for a good night's sleep. Tomorrow could be a very busy day."

Before they retired for the evening Hank downloaded Mansfield's picture from his cell phone to his laptop and printed out two large pictures on bond paper.

It was mid-morning when Hank and Helen pulled into the Driscolls' neighborhood and found a parking space right in front of Millie Hardwick's house. Millie must have been observing her visitors' arrival because Hank had barely knocked on her door one time when the door opened. Seeing Helen standing beside Hank she said, "Welcome back, dearie. Is this tall handsome man your hubby?"

Helen responded with a smile and said, "Yes, Millie, this is my husband, Hank."

"Well come on in. What brings you back to the neighborhood?" Millie asked.

"We have a photo we would like you to look at to see if it might be the man who dropped off Mr. Driscoll's boat back in October," Helen answered.

"Well, I don't know, but I'll take a look. Like I told you before it was a very dark night and I couldn't see much of anything."

When Hank handed the photo to Millie she looked at it a few seconds and then said, "Well, young fella, I can't say this is the man who dropped off the boat, but he has paid Mrs. Driscoll visits before and after she was widowed. I forgot all about him when I last talked with your wife."

"Are you sure about the identification?" Hank asked.

"Of course I'm sure," Millie responded. "I saw him through my eight by forty Nikon binocs that are over there on the table."

Hank and Helen both turned and saw the binoculars resting upright, ready for use, on the table by the front window.

"Millie, do you remember when you first started seeing this gentlemen visit Mrs. Driscoll?" Helen excitedly asked.

"I may have a little trouble remembering everything so that's why I write it all down in my log," Millie answered as she retrieved a spiral bound notebook from the same table that held the binoculars.

Millie paged back through the notebook and said, "Yes! Here it is. It was Thursday, the seventh of October, at five to eleven. He drove a black pickup truck with them tinted windows and pulled right up into her driveway. As I remember now, he had a white envelope in his hand when he went to her door."

"How long did he stay?" Helen asked.

"Oh, he was there a long time," Millie answered. "It was at least three hours. The truck was still there in mid-afternoon when I had to take some laundry out of the dryer. When I returned to the front window the truck was gone."

"Ms. Hardwick, did you make notes in your log of the other times this gentleman paid visits to Mrs. Driscoll?" Hank asked.

"I'm sure I did," Millie answered as she paged forward in the notebook. "Thursday, October the fourteenth at ten a.m., man in black truck visits Mrs. Driscoll." Paging a little further she said, "Sunday, October the twenty-fourth at two p.m., man in black truck visits Mrs. Driscoll."

"Hank, October the twenty-fourth was the day after you and Chip found Driscoll's body!" Helen said.

"Ms. Hardwick, the information that you just gave us is a great big help," Hank said. "Thank you very much. I am afraid we have to run off now."

As they were about to leave Millie said, "There's one more thing you might be interested in."

"What is that?" Helen asked.

"It was only a few days after that man's first visit that Mrs. Driscoll and Mr. Billings started their frequent trips across the street to each other's house," Millie replied. "With all this hanky-panky going on in the neighborhood, I've been thinkin of findin me a man."

"Millie, you have an eligible bachelor living right next door," Helen suggested.

Millie replied, "You mean old Mr. Hamby? He's way too old for me. Why, he probably doesn't remember how to do anything anyways." As she smiled at Hank she said, "I need a younger man."

"This one's taken," Helen said laughingly as she took Hank by the arm and headed out the door.

"Do you want to pay Susan Driscoll a visit since we're in the neighborhood?" Helen asked when they were seated back in the Honda.

"That might be just a little bit premature," Hank replied. "I think the best thing to do is to head back to Homer and have another session with Deputy Mansfield at the Sheriff's Office. By the way, thanks for saving me from that old cougar."

"As if you needed saving," Helen laughingly said.

Hank called ahead to Sheriff Pettibone and arranged another meeting with him and Deputy Mansfield at twelve noon. He then called Detective Meyers who had to be located in the police station. He came on the line a few minutes later. "Robbery Homicide, Detective Meyers speaking."

"Craig, this is Hank Moran."

"Hank, did you solve our murder case yet?"

"We're getting close, Craig. I'm calling to give you a heads up. We'll be talking with Sheriff Pettibone and one of his deputies in about an hour. The deputy seems to have a close relationship with Susan Driscoll. In fact, he paid her a visit the day after Driscoll's body was recovered. He might try to contact her after our meeting at noon. I think it would be a wise move to have her place watched this afternoon just in case she tries to go on an extended vacation."

"I see. You think she's involved with the murder, Hank?"

"It's starting to look that way, Craig. We'll know more after today's meeting."

"OK, Hank, I'll put a man on it after lunch."

"Thanks, Craig. I'll get back with you after the meeting."

Chapter 17

Hank and Helen were once again ushered into Sheriff Pettibone's office as the station's antique wall clock chimed twelve noon.

"Ya'll are right on time, folks," Pettibone said. "Deputy Mansfield will be along in a minute. Now, tell me what this is all about."

Hank told the sheriff about Mansfield's acquaintance with Susan Driscoll and about his frequent visits to her house. Sheriff Pettibone was extremely interested in Mansfield's visit to her house the day after the discovery of her husband's body. "I am sure his visit wasn't for the purpose of offering her the department's condolences," Pettibone said. "The Shreveport Police Department took care of that."

There was a knock on the sheriff's door and he shouted for the knocker to come in. Mansfield entered and saw the Morans once again sitting in front of his boss' desk. "What now?" he said under his breath.

"Deputy Mansfield, you know the routine. Pull up a chair and have a seat," Pettibone said.

After Mansfield was seated the sheriff began. "Deputy Mansfield, these good people have uncovered a few tidbits about a relationship you appear to have with Mrs. Susan Driscoll, and you better have a darn good explanation for them. Mr. Moran, you can go ahead and present your findings."

Hank began by saying, "Deputy Mansfield, we have a witness that will swear that you visited Leonard Driscoll's wife, Susan, three times during the month of October. Your first visit was on October the seventh. Susan Driscoll greeted you at the door and you entered her house carrying a white envelope. You were there for a period of about three hours. Your second visit was a week later and your third visit was the day after her husband's body was pulled from Lake Claiborne."

Mansfield had no verbal response to Hank's accusation. He sat there with a look of defeat on his face and just stared at the edge of the sheriff's desk.

Sheriff Pettibone broke the silence and said, "Deputy Mansfield, I want to know what you were doing associating with a man's wife just weeks before he was murdered and the day after his dead body was found. You have been a deputy sheriff long enough to realize that you are now a top suspect in the man's murder, especially since you were in the park at the opportune time."

Mansfield closed his eyes and sat with his elbows on his knees and his face in his hands. After a moment he said, "Sir, I guess I'm gonna have to come clean on this whole affair before that bitch tries to put the whole thing on me."

"By 'that bitch' I assume you are talking about Susan Driscoll?" Pettibone asked, eyeing a silent apology to Helen.

"Yes, sir," Mansfield responded. "I better start at the beginning."

Sheriff Pettibone opened a side drawer on his desk and pulled out a digital recorder, turned it on, and placed it on his desk in front of Mansfield and said, "Go ahead, son."

Mansfield started his story:

"A few months ago, I saw Lucy in the parking lot of the Chamber of Commerce building and asked her for a date. She turned me down as usual but this time she said she was seeing someone else. She just said it was someone from Shreveport and wouldn't tell me his name.

"Out of curiosity, I watched her house the next evening and took photographs of the man and his truck. I ran his tags and found out his name and after that discovered that he was married and was over ten years her senior. I realized that Lucy had no feelings for me besides just being friends but I still had feelings for her. I thought she was doing the wrong thing by dating Leonard Driscoll and that she would eventually be hurt by the relationship, so I decided to try to do something about it.

"I took some more photos of the two of them together both at her house and over in Shreveport at a casino. I kept the photos on my computer for over a month while I was on call for that big burglary ring case. After that case was closed I had a few days comp time coming so I called Mrs. Driscoll and made an appointment to see her. I printed the dozen pictures and stuffed them into a white envelope. When she looked at the pictures she wasn't upset at all—in fact, she more or less seduced me and we wound up in her bedroom.

"She called me a week later and asked me to come over again, so I did. I didn't see her again until about a week later when I rode my bike to the park. I had called Leonard earlier that day and we agreed on a time for me to see his boat that he had for sale. When I arrived at the boat dock I saw Susan and her husband arguing. He was standing in his boat and she was standing on the dock. She glanced my way and I nodded as I drove on past. I didn't want to stop and get involved so I just kept on going to the bike trails.

"About a half hour later, my cell phone rang and it was Susan. She said she needed my help down by the boat ramp. When I got back to the ramp I saw that she had Leonard's truck and boat trailer backed partially down the ramp. I asked her where her husband was and she said he got mad and took off on foot down the road. She said that he told her he was getting another ride and that she could have the damn boat and the truck. I figured that he had called Lucy to pick him up.

"She didn't want to leave the boat and truck there overnight so she asked me if I could help her trailer the boat and drive it back to Shreveport since she had her own car to drive back. I trailered the boat and as I was pulling the rig up the ramp my cell phone rang. It was the office calling me in to help with the hostage situation at the courthouse. I told her to go on ahead home and that I would drive the rig back to Shreveport later that night. She agreed and left and I put my bike in the back of Leonard's truck and drove to my late mother's place where my truck was parked.

"I drove the rig to Leonard's house later that night and rode my bike back home. The following Sunday when I found out that it was Leonard Driscoll's body that was found in the lake I was floored. I realized that Susan was most likely responsible for her husband's death. I immediately called her and asked what in hell was going on. She asked me to come over to Shreveport and said she would explain the whole thing when I got there.

"When I arrived at her house she calmly told me what had happened. She said when Wednesday's mail arrived she opened a letter that Leonard's attorney had sent him. The letter included papers for her husband to sign to start divorce proceedings. She got angry and drove immediately to Lake Claiborne. When she arrived at the boat dock Leonard was preparing to go out into the lake.

"She told him about finding the letter and they started arguing. Leonard convinced her to get into the boat so they could discuss things in more privacy out on the lake. As they were motoring away from the dock Leonard called his brother to inform him about a delivery that had to be made the next day.

"Leonard stopped the boat when they reached a small cove and they started arguing again. Leonard became irate and slapped Susan across the face when she told him that Lucy was nothing more than a gold digging little slut. Leonard was slightly off balance from the rocking boat after he slapped her. Then in a rage at being hit by her husband, she picked up a wooden oar, swung it, and hit Leonard on the side of the head. He immediately fell to the small deck of the boat and lay there bleeding. She panicked when she thought she had killed him. She found a knife in Leonard's tackle box, cut the anchor rope loose from the boat, wrapped it around his body a few times, rolled him overboard, and pitched the anchor in after him. As he was being pulled under by the anchor she saw his eyes open and look up at her. He struggled somewhat, but he kept sinking. He was soon out of sight.

"She thought she could make it look like an accident by leaving the boat adrift near the cove and walking back on the fire trail to the parking lot, but then she remembered that I saw her at the dock. That's when she called me for help, as I told you previously.

"She then threatened if I told anyone what she did, she would testify I was in the boat with them, and I was the

151

one who had murdered Leonard. It would have been her word against mine. She is a very convincing woman and I thought the police would believe her over me. That's why I didn't say anything all this time."

When Mansfield completed his story Pettibone asked, "Did you have any further dealings or conversations with Susan Driscoll after that Sunday?"

"No, sir, she called me a few days later, but I didn't answer the phone and she didn't leave a message. That may have been after she received the results of the coroner's findings that the actual cause of Leonard's death was drowning. Her husband was still alive when she rolled him overboard. I don't think that news would have fazed her one way or the other."

"Deputy Mansfield, you must realize that even if you are innocent of the murder, you will still be charged with obstruction of justice and withholding evidence in a murder investigation. I can't let you walk out of here, son. Hand over your weapon and badge. You will be held in a cell here at the station while we get Mrs. Driscoll's side of the story. Formal charges will be made after that time. Follow me."

Pettibone led Mansfield out of his office and escorted him to a cell in the rear of the building. Hank and Helen were still seated when he returned to his office. "Well, folks, we need to place a call to the Shreveport P.D. and have them pick up the not-so-grieving widow Driscoll."

Hank said, "I placed a call to Detective Meyers when we were on the way over here and made a request for someone to watch her house in case she decided to leave town. I can call him now and have her picked up."

"Be my guest," Pettibone replied.

Hank put his phone in speaker mode and punched Meyers' number on his speed dial. This time the detective answered on the second ring. "Meyers here."

"Craig, this is Hank. You need to pick up Susan Driscoll for the murder of her husband."

"Will do, Hank, but first you need tell me what brought you to that conclusion."

"We just heard a testimony by Claiborne Parish Deputy Sheriff Richard Mansfield, who stated that Susan Driscoll confessed to the murder to him on Sunday the twenty-fourth of October. Mrs. Moran and I and Sheriff Pettibone were present. The testimony was recorded by Sheriff Pettibone."

"You said that she confessed to a deputy sheriff nearly two months ago? What happened that he is just telling you this now?" Meyers asked.

"It's a long story, Craig. I'll fill you in when we get there in a little over an hour."

"OK, Hank, we'll have Mrs. Driscoll waiting in the interview room when you get here."

Detective Meyers arose from his desk and greeted Hank and Helen when they walked into the Shreveport Detective Division office exactly one hour after making their call.

"Hank, Mrs. Moran, please have a seat and bring me up to date before I begin questioning Susan Driscoll," Meyers said.

"Did she give you any trouble when you picked her up?" Hank asked.

"No, no trouble at all. In fact she was very cooperative when we asked her to accompany us to the station for questioning. She said she was anxious to tell what happened so that she could get back home in time for her bridge club meeting."

"Sounds like she is full of confidence," Helen said.

"The last time that I passed by the interview room she was calmly sipping on a cup of coffee. Now, fill me in on the deputy sheriff's testimony so we can get on with this," Meyers said.

Hank retold Mansfield's story including Susan Driscoll's alleged confession that was made to the deputy.

"Well, that's quite a story," Meyers said. I can't wait to hear Mrs. Driscoll's side of it. You two can watch through the one-way glass if you'd like."

"We wouldn't miss it," Hank replied.

Susan Driscoll put down her coffee cup when Detective Meyers entered the interview room.

Meyers said, "I'm sorry that I had to keep you waiting so long, Mrs. Driscoll, but we were waiting for additional information to arrive from Claiborne Parish before we could talk to you."

"That's OK, Detective. I enjoyed the cup of coffee," Susan calmly replied.

"Mrs. Driscoll, you need to know that our conversation is being recorded both on audio and video."

"Whatever is your pleasure, Detective."

"Mrs. Driscoll, the Claiborne Parish Sheriff has a recorded statement made by one of his deputies, by the name of Richard Mansfield, alleging that on October the twenty-fourth you confessed to him that you were the person who murdered your husband Leonard Driscoll."

"Of course he would say that. He's a dammed liar. He's just trying to save his own neck," Susan angrily replied.

"You didn't make a confession to him?" Meyers asked.

"Of course not. Why would I confess to something that he did?"

"Mrs. Driscoll, perhaps you should tell us your side of the story beginning on the day that Deputy Mansfield visited your house and showed you the pictures of your husband and Lucy Chatham."

"Ah, the pictures, yes, that is a good place to start."

"Please go ahead, Mrs. Driscoll."

"A few weeks before he murdered my husband, Deputy Mansfield came to my house, while Leonard was at the store, to show me some pictures he took of Leonard and Lucy Chatham. I viewed the photos with amusement and told him the pictures were no big deal."

"Excuse me for interrupting, Mrs. Driscoll, but weren't you upset about the pictures?" Meyers asked.

"Detective Meyers, my late husband and I had an open marriage for the last year and a half. We were both seeing other sexual partners. No, I was not upset with the pictures. And, please, Detective Meyers, you may call me Susan."

"Mrs. Driscoll, did Deputy Mansfield tell you why he took the pictures?" Meyers asked, making it a point to emphasize Mrs. Driscoll.

"Yes, he said that he was in love with Lucy Chatham and that he was trying to break up the relationship between her and Leonard. I explained to him that Lucy obviously did not have mutual feelings for him and that he was wasting his time pursuing her affections. He seemed to come to his senses then because we spent the next three hours in my bedroom."

"When did you next have contact with Deputy Mansfield?" Meyers asked.

"I invited him to the house about a week later," Susan answered.

"And what was the purpose of that visit?"

"You may just use your imagination, Detective," Susan answered smiling with a provocative look directly into Meyers' eyes.

Meyers momentarily lost his composure and then re-gained it by asking, "Did you have contact with Deputy Mansfield after that second meeting?"

"Yes, I did. It was on the day he killed Leonard. Soon after Leonard had left to go over to Lake Claiborne to show his boat to a prospective buyer, the mailman delivered a letter from his attorney. Being naturally curious, I opened it and saw that Leonard was starting divorce proceedings. This was obviously not part of our open marriage agreement, so I was upset after reading the letter and decided to drive over to the lake to confront Leonard. When I arrived at the lake, a man, who I assumed was the prospective buyer, was just leaving. I waited until he drove away and then got out of my car and walked down to the dock. Leonard looked surprised to see me and asked what I was doing there. I told him about his lawyer's letter and we started arguing. A few minutes later, Deputy Mansfield showed up on his trail bike. He said he was sorry to interrupt, but he saw the For Sale sign on the boat trailer and said he might be interested in buying the boat. I was curious to see what Deputy Mansfield was up to, so I went along for the demonstration ride out on the boat. We entered a small cove and Mansfield told Leonard to shut the motor off. Leonard asked why and Mansfield told him he just wanted to make sure it would restart. When Leonard shut the motor off Mansfield told him not to restart it because he wanted to have a nice quiet discussion with him about Lucy Chatham. Well, it turned out not to be a nice quiet discussion when Leonard told him that he planned to marry Lucy. Mansfield became irate and threatened Leonard that if he didn't break off his relationship with Lucy he would be in no shape whatsoever to marry her. Leonard then shoved Mansfield and Mansfield shoved him back, picked up an oar, and hit Leonard on the side of the head. Leonard fell unconscious onto the deck. Mansfield then cut the anchor rope from the boat and wrapped it around Leonard a few times, rolled him overboard, and threw the anchor in after him. I screamed at him saying that Leonard might still be alive. He then grabbed me by the neck and said 'He won't be alive for long.' Then he threatened me by saying that I would join Leonard if I breathed one word about what happened. He let go of my neck, started the motor, and sped out of the cove. On the way back to the dock he threw the oar overboard. After we reached the dock told me to go on home and to remember what he told me about not telling anyone. I ran to my car and drove home shaking the whole way. The next morning I saw that Leonard's truck was parked out front and the boat was down the street. I assumed that Mansfield drove the rig back to my house."

"Mrs. Driscoll, why didn't you contact the police after what happened?" Meyers asked.

"I was totally afraid to open my mouth. I kept hearing his threat and seeing the crazed look in his eyes. I knew he would kill me if I went to the police."

"Did Mansfield come to your house the day after your husband's body was found in the lake?" Meyers asked.

"Yes, he did. He came to threaten me again and said that I was being a good girl so far. This time when he threatened me he grabbed hold of my jaw and held a handgun to my head. I was terrified."

"Well, Mrs. Driscoll, that sure is an interesting story," Meyers began. "I am afraid we have to hold you overnight on obstruction of justice charges until we decide if you or Deputy Mansfield told the truth about which one of you murdered your husband."

"Why am I being held on obstruction of justice charges? I was threatened with my life!" Susan shouted.

"Mrs. Driscoll, if you would have come forward, we would have protected you from Mansfield."

"But what about my bridge meeting?" Susan asked.

"Mrs. Driscoll, you may make one phone call, Meyers answered. "It could be either to your bridge club or your lawyer. You make the choice."

Hank and Helen watched and heard the whole interview and were perplexed by Susan Driscoll's apparent sincerity. Meyers came out of the interview room and asked Hank and Helen to join him in the department's conference room. When they were seated he asked, "Well, folks, what do you think of Susan Driscoll's story?"

"Both Susan's and Deputy Mansfield's accounts sounded convincing," Hank said. "I guess it all boils down to his word against hers."

"Or there is a third possibility. What if they are both guilty and ratting on each other to save their own skins?" Meyers posed.

"That is also a possibility," Hank said, "There has to be something in their stories that we aren't seeing at the moment. We should just take some time to think about it. They are both being held and aren't going anywhere. Maybe something in their testimonies will surface and point to whichever one is guilty."

"You're right, Hank. Let's all go home."

Helen had called Ali during the drive from Homer to Shreveport and Ali insisted that they stop by for dinner before they head back to Lake Claiborne. They hadn't seen their grandson for over a week and wanted to see him before tomorrow's long drive back home to Kenner. The investigation into Leonard Driscoll's murder was now in the hands of the two police jurisdictions with one or both of the guilty people in custody. However, Hank was still perplexed that he couldn't reason which person was guilty, Susan Driscoll or Deputy Mansfield.

They swung by the Driscoll Furniture store on the way from the Shreveport Police Station to their daughter's house. Hank wanted to break the news personally to Peter Driscoll about his sister-in-law.

When Hank told Peter about the day's happenings he just sat behind his desk in amazement and shook his head.

"I can't believe that Susan could be capable of murdering Leonard. It had to be the deputy," Peter said.

Hank replied, "We know that one or both of them are guilty. From what I've seen and heard today I think either one of them was capable of the crime."

"I guess I didn't really know my sister-in-law very well or even my brother for that matter," Peter replied. "Hank, I want to thank you for your good work in finding my brother's murderer. I just didn't think it would hit this close to home though. Well, I guess your job is finished now. Preston is still helping out with the store's accounting. You can give your final invoice to him."

"I'm sorry to have had to give you the news about Susan," Hank said. "There is still the possibility that she is the innocent party."

"I'll just hope for the best," Peter replied.

Hank and Helen arrived at Ali's house and were greeted with hugs from their daughter and grandson. Preston was in the kitchen stirring the pot of spaghetti sauce and Italian meatballs to prevent the mixture from sticking to the bottom.

"We're having my favorite spaghetti and meatballs tonight, Grampa," Chip said.

"That's one of my favorites, too, and I'm really hungry. You better get yours before I eat it all up," Hank replied.

"We've got a really big potful. There's no way you could eat it all, Grampa," Chip countered.

After everyone was seated at the dinner table with full plates of spaghetti, Preston asked to hear about the arrests of Susan and the deputy. Hank thought it was a good idea to talk about it, hoping something would surface from both the testimonies that would point to the guilty person.

Hank related the day's events between mouthfuls of spaghetti while Chip listened intently. When he was finished, he ended by saying that it was Susan's word against the deputy's and it might prove very hard to figure out which one was lying.

Chip downed a mouthful of spaghetti and followed it with a drink of water and then said, "I know who was lying, Grampa."

"You do?" Hank asked with a grin. "How did you figure it out, Chip?"

"I figured it out from the cell phone call that Mrs. Driscoll made to Deputy Mansfield."

As soon as Chip mentioned the cell phone call it dawned on Helen what Chip was thinking and she said with a knowing grin, "Go on, Chip, tell us about the phone call."

"Well, why would Mrs. Driscoll call Deputy Mansfield on her cell phone if they were on the boat together?" Chip asked.

Hank just sat back dumbfounded that it took a ten year old to figure out the puzzle. He congratulated Chip and rose from the table, cell phone in hand, and dialed Detective Craig Meyers' number.

When Meyers answered the call he said, "What's up, Hank? Did you figure it out?"

"I didn't, Craig, but my ten year old grandson did. You need to check the cell phone records of both Deputy Mansfield and Susan Driscoll. If the call from Susan Driscoll to Mansfield around five-thirty on the day of the murder took place as Mansfield said it did, then Susan Driscoll is the guilty one."

Meyers replied, "Please elaborate just a little bit more, Hank, I'm afraid I'm not following you."

"Craig, as my grandson so wisely asked: 'Why would she make that call if she and Mansfield were on Leonard's boat together?'"

"Dead catch, Hank!" Meyers replied in excitement.

"I'm sorry, Craig, now I'm not following you. Dead catch?"

"Yeah, Hank, that's just a term we use here in the department for when we finally nail the perpetrator. It's short for 'catching them dead to right.'"

"It's also a good term for how this whole investigation got started."

159

"Well, Hank, it appears your grandson started it and ended it. I'll get those phone records first thing in the morning and contact Sheriff Pettibone. Thank Chip for me."

"Will do, Craig."

"Well, Hank, it looks like the investigation is over. Will you be heading back to Kenner in the morning?" Preston asked.

"I'm afraid so. By the way, Peter said that I should submit my final invoice to you," Hank said.

"Just send it on up and I'll handle it," Preston replied.

"We do need to get back home. I have to catch up on the yard work and do a little painting on the house. We also have to look into the possibility of adding a room onto the house for an office. Now that I have a partner, we'll need the extra space."

"You didn't tell us that you had a partner for your agency," Ali said.

"I didn't? Well, meet my new partner in the Moran Investigations Agency. Mrs. Moran, please stand up."

"Mother?" Ali replied.

"That's right, dear. I'll be starting the process to obtain my license as soon as we get home. In fact, we'll be going right through Baton Rouge on the way home, so we might as well stop and start the paperwork."

"Mother, you're incorrigible!"

EPILOGUE

While Detective Meyers was waiting for the phone company to forward the record of calls made on Susan Driscoll's and Deputy Mansfield's cell phones made on October the twentieth, he called Sheriff Pettibone. He asked the sheriff if Deputy Mansfield's cell phone was near at hand and to check it for a record of an incoming call from Susan Driscoll's phone on the day of the murder. Meyers then gave the sheriff Susan Driscoll's cell phone number. He would have verified the call on Susan Driscoll's phone but she had recently deleted her call record. After Meyers explained why he needed the information, Pettibone said he would call him back in ten minutes.

Pettibone called back and said that a record of the call was still present on Mansfield's phone. The call took place at exactly 5:27 p.m. Knowing that the records from the phone company would show the same call, Meyers didn't wait until he received those records and formally charged Susan Driscoll for the murder of her husband. She was then held as a flight risk without bail at the female detention center.

Deputy Mansfield was relieved from duty as a deputy sheriff and was released from jail on his own recognizance pending possible charges contemplated by the District Attorney.

Helen's application for an apprentice license in the Moran Investigations Agency was approved and Hank was successful in obtaining a building permit for the addition of an office to the Moran residence.

They made a trip back up to Shreveport for Christmas dinner and the exchanging of gifts at Ali's house.

Chip gave a disappointed look when Hank handed him a small wrapped gift. His disappointment quickly turned to joy when he unwrapped the package and found a bright, shiny junior detective's badge for the Moran Investigations Agency. Hank had the badge specially made and it arrived just two days before Christmas. Hank assured Chip that he would be the agency's chief consultant whenever they had a tough case to crack. The badge found a permanent place on Chip's pants belt, the same place his Grampa Hank wore his.

About the Author

L.D. Knorr was born and raised on a dairy farm in Berks County Pennsylvania and now resides in rural Alabama. His profession as a mechanical engineer required his relocation from Pennsylvania to Mississippi, Texas, and Alabama. He honed his writing skills on engineering related technical papers and reports. Now being retired he is focusing his attention on fiction.

He has been married fifty years to his wife Emily and they were blessed with three talented and creative children. They have also had their own adventures traveling the country in their RV.

www.ingramcontent.com/pod-product-compliance
Lightning Source LLC
Chambersburg PA
CBHW070036260626
47159CB00005B/2055